A DISH
BEST
SERVED
COLD?

A DISH BEST SERVED COLD?

CHRIS KINSEY

Matador
Unit E2 Airfield Business Park,
Harrison Road, Market Harborough,
Leicestershire. LE16 7UL
Tel: 0116 279 2299
Email: books@troubador.co.uk
Web: www.troubador.co.uk/matador
Twitter: @matadorbooks

ISBN 978 180313 674 5

British Library Cataloguing in Publication Data.
A catalogue record for this book is available from the British Library.

Printed and bound in the UK by TJ Books Limited, Padstow, Cornwall
Typeset in 11pt Minion Pro by Troubador Publishing Ltd, Leicester, UK

Matador is an imprint of Troubador Publishing Ltd

MIX
Paper from
responsible sources
FSC® C013056

To my ever patient, long enduring, gorgeous Hils x
You always believed that I'd get it finished x

CHAPTER ONE
The Beginning 1985

Sonny Wilton stood rigid with fear. He looked down the hallway into the kitchen. Both his parents were screaming at each other.

Sonny had witnessed many arguments throughout his short life, but this one was different. On Thursday evening his mother had escaped to the local pub, not returning to the house until Sunday morning.

The atmosphere across the weekend had been tense, with Sonny's father sitting by the phone, waiting for a call. As Friday turned into Saturday, Sonny could feel the humiliation boil up inside his father. This time she had been gone three days!

Then, as bold as brass, his mother had just wandered back in with a look that said, 'And what are you gonna do about it?' This was goading an already savage animal to say the least.

Jimmy, who had been carving up a poor excuse for a Sunday joint, threw the gravy dish across the room, missing his wife by an inch.

The radio in the small kitchen was weirdly playing *Wild boys* by Duran Duran in the background of the horrid, toxic scene. Sonny watched as his unshaven father stabbed the meat over and over again in blind fury. He didn't seem to be aware that he was holding the knife in his hand.

'I will not ask you again, Wend. Where have you been?' His father pointed the blade straight at his stern-looking wife.

'Oh, you know. Out and about!' His mother, ever defiant and unrepentant, crossed her arms.

"Cos, you see, I searched everywhere for you. Where the fuck have you been?'

His father made a deliberate step towards his wife.

His mother did not flinch. 'What have I told you about spying on me when I'm out with my bloody friends?' She pointed a mocking, accusing finger at her husband, totally unaware of the impending horror that she was encouraging.

'All your ugly, scumbag friends haven't seen you for the last two nights. So, where were you? And who the fuck were you with? For three… fucking… nights!'

Sonny edged into the kitchen. His father's eyes said it all. Something terrible was about to happen.

'I'm leaving you, Jimmy.'

Sonny clasped his hands over his eyes. This was going to end badly.

'There, I've said it, at last.' There was a determined and final tone in his mother's voice.

'You're leaving *me*! I've not looked at another woman in the last twelve fucking years. You, on the other hand, have been on your back for any idiot who'll buy you half a lager. And you're leaving me! You really take the piss, Wend. I'll tell you something. You'd be dead before you were out the door.' He slammed the knife into the table to emphasise his intent.

His mother edged towards his father and offered a mocking laugh.

'You haven't got what it takes, you bastard. Who do you think you are? Your father? You ain`t a quarter of the man he is, or a quarter of the man I've been with the last three nights. The man I'm leaving you for.'

Sonny crept into the room. 'But, Mum. You can't leave me here?'

'Try me. I'm sure you'll both be happy.'

'I'm fucking warning you, Wendy. I *am fucking* warning you,' his father shouted, his eyes wide open in uncontrollable rage. He held the knife so tight that his fingers were ghostly white.

'Go on then, you spineless fucker!' screamed his mother as she stood in front of her fuming husband. She opened her arms, almost encouraging the violence.

Sonny couldn't bear to watch and clasped his fingers over his eyes. He listened as his father thrust the knife deep into his mother's chest. He heard his mother scream, and edged backwards in fear. He opened his eyes and watched as his father stepped back as well.

His father seemed to be morbidly transfixed as his wife's head started to nod up and down in shock. Sonny felt every muscle in his body tighten as a circle of blood appeared on his mother's chest. His mother lifted one hand and touched the handle of the knife almost tenderly, and then fell backwards, her legs folding awkwardly beneath her. She didn't close her eyes to embrace death. In truth, Wendy Wilton was very much dead before she had hit the floor.

Sonny edged backwards. His father was now sporting a demented, twisted grin. He seemed to be curiously surveying the gruesome spectacle he had created. He reached down and gripped the handle of the carving knife embedded in his wife's chest, and slowly withdrew it from her body. There was a soft sucking and grating against bone as his mother's body gave up the blade.

His father turned his attention to Sonny, who stood trembling, his young eyes transfixed on his mother's body, a pool of blood growing around her. Sonny no longer recognised his father, as a sadistic smile chilled his blood. He beckoned to his son. 'Sonny. Come here, Sonny. Come here, Sonny!' He held the knife by his side and laughed – an under the breath kind of laugh – where only air comes out, with no sound. 'Come here, Sonny!' There was urgency in the voice.

Sonny stood rooted to the spot. Still trembling. 'Come here, you little bastard. I'm gonna send you off to join that dirty whore!' He kicked the body so hard that his mother turned over and her dead glassy eyes looked straight at Sonny.

This snapped the boy out of his paralysed trance. 'Come here, Sonny boy. Come and fucking die for Daddy!'

Sonny spun around, in total terrified panic. He dashed towards the front door. As he fumbled with the latch, his father reached out, his face twisted in rage. He seemed to be oblivious to anything, but the intention to plunge the knife into his own son. He didn't even see the vacuum cleaner lying on the floor and tripped over it, his balance completely thrown. As he crashed to the floor, the knife entered his right eye with a sickening pop.

Sonny watched as his father convulsed, the blood pouring

down his face. He winced, realising that the blade had gone right into his father's brain. Sonny fumbled with the door handle and swung the door open.

*

Mrs Hill lived next door to the Wilton's and was only too aware of Wendy's infidelities. As she stood in the garden, looking over the fence, she attempted to gather some trashy gossip for the headscarf and rollers brigade that occupied the window corner at the Vauxhall. She would have offered her help in the past, but not anymore. As far as she was concerned this was all the fault of Alf Wilton.

'King of the fucking coal, isn't he?' she said to her husband. 'Shame he can't keep his daughter-in-law, and her loose bloody drawers, in check. It's that poor little lad I feel for, having to go through this every bloody day.' 'Just leave it, Marie. It's their problem. If it needs sorting, Alf will sort it,' her husband said.

Little Sonny Wilton hurtled down the garden path, screaming in terror. This spurned Mrs Hill into action. She grabbed the young boy and cradled him in her arms, stifling his screams in her bosom.

'Vic. Vic. Victor! I'm telling you now. That's it. Enough's enough. You bloody well get in there and sort that gutless bastard out!'

'What the fuck is going on now, woman?' he bellowed.

'What? Are you blind? Look at the boy!'

Vic leapt the small fence separating the two houses and tried the side door. He was in the house for no more than twenty seconds.

As he stumbled out of the door he retched up his breakfast over the Wilton's front lawn.

'Bloody hell, Vic! What? What? What's happened?' 'Oh, Jesus fucking Christ, Marie, call the police, ambulance, the bloody lot!'

Mrs Hill lifted the boys head from her chest and looked into his terrified eyes, 'Oh, Sonny boy, tell your Auntie Marie what's just happened?'

A veil of horror had fallen across him. He did not speak. In fact it was almost eighteen months before he spoke again.

CHAPTER TWO
Alf Wilton

Alfred James Wilton was twenty when he first became the king of the coal. Willy Crossley, who held the great position before him, had given Bethany Taylor a good beating one Saturday evening after she had spurned his advances toward her.

This led to Alfred challenging Crossley to a traditional stand-up fist fight on top of Mynydd Du (The Black Mountain).

There was an ulterior motive to the beating as far as Willy Crossley was concerned. It wasn't just her turning down his romantic intentions. Word had got around that Alfie Wilton was building a reputation as a potential leader of men.

But not women!

Alfred was shy with the opposite sex and had yet to make his feelings known to Bethany Taylor, but nothing worked better than the local bush telegraph; where Willy Crossley had taken the opportunity to goad the young upstart to the fight as a matter of honour.

Mountain boxing is basically a stand-up fight between two men stripped to the waist, wearing no more than bandages to protect their fists. A huge crowd of cheering, smoking, swearing, bloodthirsty and, most importantly, men made up the crowd. There were no rounds, there were no rules, and only a total submission or unconsciousness could produce a winner.

After the great depression of the 1920s mountain boxing became hugely popular in the pit villages of Wales. It became an easy way to make money, by either taking part in the fights, or watching the crowd throw in their small change or 'buttons' for a good display (hence the saying, Being paid in buttons) or by gambling on the fights.

It was after World War II that the king of the coal became an established and respected title amongst the Welsh communities and with it came respect, from all directions and all communities. Paying for a pint became a thing of the past. Every morning there would be fresh milk and bread on your doorstep. The butcher would make sure you got the best cuts of meat. There would always be a free appointment at the doctor's or dentist or assistance for any other such ailments that would burden the great man, and the gratuity would, of course, be extended to the wife of the champion, who would get her yards of material for making clothes, food and ingredients, and any other such necessities free of charge. Of course, the king of the coal was expected to be a leader of men, an organiser, and a chief of all the communities if you like.

A wife, whose husband was beating on her and spending his weekly wage on the horses, in the pub or letting his family go hungry, would pay a visit to the great man. He would then, in turn, visit – with a few trusted associates – the wayward husband and show him the error of his ways.

A mother, whose son had done a spell in prison for some

misdemeanour, would ask the king of coal to keep him on the straight and narrow.

A father of a daughter, who had got herself in the family way, would ask the king of the coal to convince the young lothario to do the right thing. If you like, he was the smaller, Welsh equivalent of an Italian godfather.

There were, of course, incidents that were a little foul of the law to say the least. For instance, a lorry of cigarettes, or designer clothes, hijacked off a lay-by, or lorry park, and the cargo sold to contacts in London, Manchester or Birmingham. Or the odd bank or security van robbery.

A large chunk of all monies accrued from the stolen contraband, or armed robberies, would be distributed amongst the widows of miners, or other needy families, so there was a little good done even after a bit of skulduggery had been committed.

After the beating he inflicted on Willy Crossley, Alfie Wilton became the subject of folklore. People would later say that Alfie Wilton stretched the fight out on purpose, so he could inflict as much pain on his opponent as possible.

People remembered that when Alfie Wilton finally stood over the unconscious Willy Crossley (who would from that day talk with a permanent slur and walk with a limp) his face was totally unmarked. As the baying crowd looked on their new champion they all knew that this man, all of twenty years old, was going to be a leader for a very long time.

Everybody was glad to see the back of Willy Crossley. He had been nothing but a bully, who had used his position to line his own and his cronies' pockets for years. Extorting protection money from all the local businesses and hostelries, and bedding any woman who was impressed by the tough, would-be-gangster.

It was inevitable that the now new king of the coal: community leader, people's gangster or godfather would court and eventually marry Bethany Taylor.

A few months after the great fight, all the communities came together for the big day. Bethany or Beth as she was always known (and always would be) proved that she was utterly devoted to her husband. She worshipped him with a passion that knew no bounds, from stitching his cuts and bathing his fighting wounds, to providing him with cast iron alibis when the police came calling. There was nothing she would not do for her husband. He had fought for her honour and gone onto marry her. For that she felt she owed him everything.

As for Alf, he put his wife on a pedestal, providing her with everything she wanted. Despite the fact that she was the most under demanding wife a man could ever want, he was always overwhelmed at how much he loved this woman. He bit his tongue when Beth announced she wanted to take up a position in the local nursery. Alf Wilton was an old-fashioned soul and believed a wife's position should be at home and be taken care of. This was all forgotten when he saw how much joy his wife got from providing the first steps of learning for the local small children.

But Beth would only present her husband with one child of their own, after an extremely difficult pregnancy, spending the last two months confined to bed. It was thanks to the vicious beating from Willy Crossley that she would never be able to conceive again. James Wilton came into the world during their third year of marriage. He had a happy and quite normal childhood and his parents loved him dearly. Brought up in a house where hardly a cross word was ever spoken. Alf Wilton's word was law in his own house and despite his reputation as hard, he was nothing but fair. The young boy went to the local school and was more or less an ordinary student.

It was when James Wilton reached his mid-teens that the changes in the boy became uglier, where he used the Wilton name for his own self-gain. He wasn't exactly a weedy adolescent, but nowhere near the fantastic six-foot prize fighters' physique of his father and was never ever going to be. But that didn't stop him picking fights with whomever he didn't like the look of or who wouldn't bow to the Wilton name. More often than not these opponents would not fight to their true potential for fear of reprisals.

His son's selfish attitude annoyed his father no end, but despite the long lectures the behaviour only escalated as James Wilton got older.

Walking into shops and supermarkets and out again with whatever he liked without paying became common practice. His parting comment to the proprietor would be, 'Go see the king, he'll put you straight.' He would sit in a pub or club and start a tab off in his father's name and would drink all day and into the night. Sauntering off leaving the landlord with a large bill which would be delivered to Wilton senior, along with a complaint to please try and put a stop to his son's behaviour.

A lot of James Wilton's misdemeanors went unreported, either to his father or to the police, which only encouraged him to get away with more. He thought of himself as more of a gangster than his father ever was.

In fact, he was nothing more than a leech, carrion, profiting from a reputation that he had contributed nothing to.

His behaviour completely baffled and depressed both his parents. Their son was very much loved and as far as they were concerned his upbringing had been no different to any of his school friends. His fathers' business dealings were never discussed in front of his wife or son. Ever! Criminal or legitimate activities were done in the back office of the house. Any of the men who loyally served Alf Wilton were forbidden to talk about their goings on until they were alone.

James Wilton was twenty years old when he quickly married Wendy Lewis with the nearly nine months of arms and legs thrashing around in her belly.

By the time of this great union, Alf and Beth Wilton were heartbroken to finally admit their defeat in trying to get their son to see the error of his ways and was by now lost to them. The shopkeepers, landlords and other proprietors of the communities had been given the blessing of Alf Wilton to turn his son away unless he showed the colour of his money. If they just didn't like the look of him, to turn him away anyway. James Wilton was reduced to taking handouts from his father, which he wasn't shy in doing. The three jobs his father had secured for him through various contacts hadn't lasted longer than two weeks because of either his thieving or because he hadn't bothered to show up.

The new wife of the young Wilton was the slut daughter of a slut mother and a drunken father. She had been passed around every likely lad within a ten-mile radius. She thought she was going to do alright for herself by getting her filthy, varnished and chipped fingernails into the son of the local godfather, and he must have thought he had got himself a nice catch. After all, she was a bit of a looker and popular with all the lads in the pubs. In fact, they very much deserved each other. They made a suitable couple.

Rhyston 'Sonny' (Sunny) Wilton came kicking and screaming into the world two weeks after the disaster bound marriage. He weighed a hefty ten pounds four ounces. He would continue putting on the weight week in week out, but not in fat. He was perfectly honed even as a baby and would grow to be fabulously fit and healthy with a body that was built for athletic strength. He hardly ever had a day's illness. It seemed almost impossible that he came from the seed of Jimmy Wilton, but with the shock of black hair and identical facial features the question of lineage was never going to be in dispute, and coupled with the superb male physique and strength that he seemed to be born with it was plainly obvious, he was a Wilton. His mother hated him from the very day he was born.

Alf Wilton made sure his grandson was taken care of by continuing his handouts of cash to his son (which suited Jimmy as he could cream a little off for himself). There were of course Alf's eyes and ears on the streets that would keep him in the know as to the welfare of his grandson. The young Wilton's thankfully were not that stupid as to neglect the grandchild of the great man. The grandparents would also make sure they were regular visitors to the house whether they were welcome or not. Wendy Wilton could be more than a little shy when it came to keeping the nest clean, so Beth would go round once a week and give the place a going over, and it gave her a chance to play with her grandson for a bit.

Wendy had no time for "the greedy little fucker". She would constantly moan about how much food he could put away. 'He just eats and eats,' she would moan from her armchair, where she sat chain smoking and reading the latest trashy magazines, while her mother-in-law busied herself putting a little cleanliness into the house.

It wasn't long before Wendy went back to slumming it around the pubs and disappearing for a day here and a couple of days there with her, "Girlfriends".

Sonny spent a lot of weekends with his grandparents who loved him deeply, and he loved the attention they gave him. Something that was so lacking in his own home. But , on the one Sunday that his parents met their grisly demise, he was there to witness it.

After a week at the local hospital, where he was kept an eye on until social services were happy for him to be released, the doctors concluded that he would speak again, 'In his own good time.' His grandparents naturally made the necessary and legal moves to become the guardians of the boy. He was to live with them from then on.

CHAPTER THREE
Sonny's Return

For the next twelve months there was no major event for the Wilton's, though as far as Alf and his businesses were concerned there was trouble brewing. Alf was aware that he wasn't getting any younger. His attitude on drugs was old-fashioned. His mantra had, and would always be, 'We're having nothing to do with them. If I find out 'bout anybody using, buying, dealing, borrowing or fucking stealing drugs in the name of the Wilton crew, I swear they will wish they hadn't been born.'

And when Alf Wilton made a threat it was taken as gospel law, and that was that. Violence was the last resort as far as he was concerned! A nice friendly warning always seemed to work, with impending violent repercussions not even mentioned. But if a troublemaker got out of hand, he would be swiftly picked up, driven to a secluded place, where a beating of catastrophic proportions would be meted out.

But Alf was now in his mid-fifties, and was getting fed up with the business. He wanted to find someone who had at least a thin, but genuine vein of good in them. Kelvin Harvey and Myron Vincent had been at his side for years. He trusted them with his life, but they weren't the brightest stars in the sky and, if truth be told, were getting on themselves – same era, same thinking!

The younger generation saw the combined power of the Wilton name and drugs as the way forward. Alf didn't want his business turned ugly and ruined in the name of narcotics, and would, therefore, 'Hold on and see what happens.'

*

It took Sonny a long time to come out of his shell. His grandparents took advice from social services and kept him away from the funerals.

But even though he wouldn't speak, the memory of that awful day soon faded. Somehow he pushed it into the dark recesses of his mind; possibly locked away for future nightmares.

On the advice of a child psychologist, Alf and Beth sent him to the local comprehensive, where they thought that even though he wasn't speaking, he would still be able to cope with schoolwork. As far as the classroom capabilities were concerned, they were indeed correct, but Sonny's self-imposed silence inevitably attracted the attention of bullies. He would often arrive home bruised or with a thick lip and, if questioned by his grandparents, he would just shrug his shoulders and give that resigned look that says, 'It's OK. No problem!' But every dog has his day, and Sonny Wilton's day came strangely with another piece of history visiting upon the Wilton family.

*

Samuel Crossley, the grandson of the infamous Willy Crossley, had all his life been fed the story of how Alfred

Wilton had beaten his grandpa to within an inch of his life. As a result, Sam Crossley had made it his mission to torture the mute Sonny Wilton whenever the two boy's paths would cross. Samuel, who was two years older, had kept up his promise with a nasty enthusiasm, but things were about to change.

One Friday afternoon Sonny slipped out of the gates unaware that Sam Crossley and his mates were just behind him, ready to have their fun.

'Where you going, Wilton, you dumb little fucker?' shouted Sam, his scruffy school cronies giggling behind him. This seemed to encourage the tormentor.

'You fucking deaf as well as dumb, Wilton, you weird little shit?' Sam nudged one of his mates next to him and gave him a wink that said, *Am I the mutt's nuts or what?*

Sonny carried on walking, doing his best to ignore the pack of hyenas, but he knew from previous experience that this was only heading in one direction.

Sam then snorted up into his nostrils, loud and theatrically so everyone knew what he was about to do, and spat a lump of sticky phlegm onto the back of Sonny's head. Sonny momentarily flinched in his horror, then carried on walking. He was better than this bully. He just wanted to avoid confrontation. *Why did I come this way*? he thought. *Big mistake!*

Sam did it again. This time the phlegm dribbled down the back of Sonny's neck.

Sonny felt something at the pit of his stomach. A knot of anger! The knot forced its way up into his chest, getting bigger and more violent, turning into white hot rage.

'Big mistake, Wilton. Big *fucking* mistake!' Sam poked

Sonny in the back, jabbing him painfully between the shoulder blades as they entered the wooded area of the common.

Sonny was now all on his own, but this time something had snapped inside his head. He stopped, dropped his school bag, and turned to face his tormentor. Sam appeared confused for a second, but stared at Sonny, his eyes distant and malevolent.

'What the fuck you doing, Dumbo? You wanna have a go with me, yeah?' he whispered, the spit dribbling down his mouth. He shoved Sonny, who stumbled backwards, tripped over his school bag and landed on his backside. This raised howls of laughter from the inevitable jeering crowd.

Sonny picked himself up slowly and faced up to the bully, his shoulders visibly rising and falling as he sucked in huge amounts of air.

'Your whole family are bastard mental, Wilton,' said Sam who took off his parka jacket and handed it to a crony. The crowd formed a large circle, in readiness of the inevitable thrashing of the younger boy. 'I mean, look at your old man! Stabbed your mam to death with a kitchen knife, then stuck it in his own eye. What a fucking dope! What was that all about, hey?'

Sonny's mind was racing; memories of that day crashing in and out of his subconscious.

'And *you* wanna go a few rounds with *me*? You're truly not right in the head, Wilton!' Sam looked down at Sonny with intent and menace. 'I'm gonna batter the living shit outta you, dumb boy.'

The first blow – when it came – was a slap. It caught Sonny across his left ear and sent him spinning to the floor with a ringing in his head, and a distant sound of cheering from the crowd. He rolled away from his opponent to give himself a few moments of recovery. He stood back up as a calm feeling surged through his body, a feeling that everything was under control. He then smiled.

Sam momentarily frowned in confusion. He quickly swung a punch at Sonny and it connected with a loud smack to the cheek. Sonny went down again. This was followed by a hard kick to the stomach. As far as Crossley was concerned this was enough to finish off the young boy, but the retaliation was devastating.

Sam stood in front of Sonny, his feet spread apart, his arms folded; the classic, victorious in combat stance. Once again he snorted up into his nostrils. He turned to the crowd.

'Shall I?' he shouted. The crowd jeered.

But before he could release the phlegm, Sonny launched himself like a coiled spring, and with the lower palm of his hand, he hit the bully right under his nose, breaking it with a sickening crunch.

Sam staggered back in shock, the phlegm mixed with blood dripping down his chin. Before he could assess the damage, a second punch landed perfectly – again on his now very broken nose! He screamed out in agony and dropped to his knees. The blood now flowed freely, dripping off his chin and soaking into his shirt. He had never been hurt this badly before and was petrified as to how severe his injury was. He started to blub out loud. The crowd fell silent. A young boy pointed at Sam's trousers. 'Look that boy's wet himself!' he shouted, and the crowd screamed with laughter. Humiliation indeed!

Sonny calmly bent down until he was face to face with his bloodied and defeated tormentor and grinned. He looked deep into Sam's eyes, and then calmly turned his back on the whole scene, picked up his school bag, and walked through the crowd. The rage that had burned inside him had suddenly gone. He felt calmer, almost serene. He was finally coming out of the dark place.

*

Soon, Sonny arrived at the Wilton house. It was roughly a quarter of the way up the Black Mountain. He passed through a heavy wooden gate, locked it behind him, and strolled boldly up the long garden path to the back door and into the kitchen.

Dropping his bag onto the kitchen floor, he announced in a solid and rather strong male voice, 'I'm feeling a lot better now, Grandma. Everything is going to be fine.'

*

Beth nearly threw herself under the table at the sound of this strange voice in her kitchen. She shrieked so loud that she had trouble remembering exactly what the boy had said, as she phoned her husband once the shock had worn off.

She hadn't failed to notice Sonny's dirty clothes and bruised cheek. She let it pass for now. She had chatted to him for hours with no response, so was completely speechless at these turn of events.

Sonny politely told her that he was tired and slipped out of the kitchen.

'I'm going to have a sleep,' he announced. Beth nodded blankly, feeling rather stupid.

Stupid, but elated. After almost seventeen months her grandson had found his voice.

*

Alf was disappointed when he got home. He had arrived a little later than he had hoped after driving across the county to placate one of his Asian customers, who felt he had been overcharged for some fake designer trainers. The poor bloke had indeed been ripped off and Alf was absolutely livid. It seemed that more and more people were now making decisions without consulting him. Alf was getting sick of it. The organisation was rotten to the core and Alf wanted out.

Violence against bad payers – against anyone – was becoming the norm. It was common knowledge that he was totally against making money from drugs, but people were doing it anyway. The end was coming alright, in what shape or form Alf couldn't predict, but it was definitely coming.

Alf poked his head around the door of Sonny's room. His grandson was sleeping peacefully under the covers. Alf closed the door carefully. 'We'll have that chat in the morning, son,' he whispered.

CHAPTER FOUR
Alf and Sonny

The next morning Alf did the same thing he did every day. At 5.00am he would snap awake. There was no need for an alarm clock. It was always 5.00am. Occasionally he tried to have a lie in for an hour or so, but his body clock just didn't allow it. Beth, on the other hand, could wake up at five, be fresh to face the day by quarter past – or just turn over, go back to sleep, and wake up at nine.

Alf pulled on his tracksuit bottoms. No longer running shorts. Beth had diplomatically convinced him that his legs were too skinny for running shorts, so he had tried the tighter fitting track suit bottoms and, although he never told her, he wished that he'd discovered them long before.

He quietly crept into the kitchen for his 'wake up wash' – a splash of ice cold water on the head and shoulders. After pulling on his old trainers, he would venture outside into the cold fresh morning air to undertake his daily three-mile run – but would always stop to admire the view. Even in the winter, when it was pitch dark, the black mountain was still beautiful. It was almost as though the sights and sounds had been created exclusively for him.

Alf always ran the same route and could practically do it

blindfolded. At the top of the hill Alf had strung up a punch bag. It had taken a lot of punishment over the years, but Alf would hammer at it for almost half an hour, then skip with a frayed gym rope for another thirty minutes, and finish with an old set of free weights that he had lumped up there many years previously. As the sun came up he would catch his breath, before his three-mile run back.

Alf's training site had quite a history. It was the place where most of the mountain fights had taken place. Many men, big hard men, had fought, won and lost there. It was the same place where he himself had been victorious.

*

This morning Alf started out like every other morning. He was about two miles up the track when he had a strange feeling that he was being followed. He stopped and squinted into the darkness, then slipped his hand into his pocket for the comforting feel of the cosh that he always carried on his early morning runs. He wasn't expecting what he saw coming up the old mountain track.

'What in God's name?' he muttered.

About a half a mile behind, stripped to the waist, head down and elbows pumping and looking like he'd been running this route forever, despite his mere fourteen and a bit years, was Sonny.

Alf waited for the young boy to catch him up. Sonny stopped in front of him, put his hands on his hips and looked him straight in the eye. Not a word was spoken. They both stood facing each other, their breath frosting in the morning air. Both sweating despite the cold. The boy had spoken a few words to Beth yesterday and now he was here chasing him up a mountain.

They stayed still for a minute or so, Alf willing the boy to say something, anything. But Sonny just stood there frozen to the spot. It was almost as if they were sizing each other up.

Alf couldn't help notice the obvious athletic build of his grandson. He already had the envious triangular cut of good upper body strength and that look of determination, defiance even.

Alf nodded his head toward the top of the mountain. Sonny nodded as if in agreement and they both continued their run. Alf smiled to himself as they ran side by side. A smile of realisation; he was running next to a replica, a clone even, of himself.

When they reached the top of the mountain, which was quite flat and level, Alf sat on an old log that had served as a bench for many a year. He rested his hands on his knees, taking in deep breaths after the steep run. Sonny joined him, but remarkably, appeared to be hardly out of breath.

'This is my favourite place to be, y'know. I love to come here,' he said, not looking at his grandson, but sweeping his gaze across the makeshift open-air gym.

'I like it,' Sonny replied.

Alf smiled broadly at hearing his grandson's first words in a very long time. He felt that same parental love that he hadn't felt for an eternity. His son's downward spiral and eventual grisly demise had clouded his mind. He loved his son, always had, always would, but this was different. Maybe he was going to be given another chance.

'I've been running up here since I was your age, and my father ran it before me,' he continued.

'Did my dad ever do the run?' Sonny asked.

'No, he was never one for looking after himself.'

'He was a no good, lazy bastard. And so was she,' Sonny said with conviction as he looked his grandfather straight in the eyes.

'Son, I know you're angry and you have every right to be, but he was your father and you have to find it in your heart to forgive.'

Sonny stood and faced his grandfather and with a calmness that told Alf that the boy had obviously spent a long time reliving the horrors that he had seen.

'Never,' Sonny whispered.

Alf decided to let it go, change the conversation. 'So, you want to get yourself fit? You're in pretty good shape already for a young lad.'

'I want to learn to box, like you. Grandma showed me the pictures of you. I'm gonna learn to fight. I can do it. I can feel it in me,' Sonny said in a matter-of-factly kind of way that Alf had to nod in admiration. As a boy he could remember having the same feelings.

'And where, on top of an old mountain in Wales, are you going to find someone to help you? Someone to teach you, to train you may I ask.'

Alf looked at his grandson with raised eyebrows, but also with half a smile.

Sonny offered his grandpa a wide knowing grin. 'Then it's about time I introduced you to my very old friend, Mr Punch Bag.'

CHAPTER FIVE
Sonny the Fighter

'Tell you what, Alf. I wouldn't have taken him on in the ring, not even in my prime, absolutely no way. Not for any amount of cash – the boy is a goddamn machine.' Kelvin Harvey laughed at his own confession, as he watched Sonny repeatedly jab the pads held firm by his grandfather.

Kelvin was an old and much trusted friend of Alf's. They, with Myron Vincent, had gone to school together, fought their enemies together, committed acts of skulduggery together, and acted as best man at each other's weddings. They knew each other as only best friends could; all proud men that would lay their lives down for each other. No questions asked!

Sonny was being put through his paces in the mountain ring. His speed and power were holding the small crowd in awe. In the three years since he had decided to speak again, he had taken to the boxing training like the proverbial duck to water. His schoolwork was as average, as most students, and he had finished his fifth year at school with a few CSEs, with no desire to go to college or university. Alf had envisaged setting the boy up with his own legitimate business, but Sonny showed no interest; he was born to fight. It was his calling.

His fitness was second-to-none, but it was his hand speed and devastating power that impressed, alongside his devastating good looks; with quite a few of the young beauties seeking his attention. But Sonny only had eyes for one, the stunning Rhian Hughes, the daughter of Arthur Hughes, the local newsagent. They had gone to school together, and Rhian had been really supportive when Sonny did not speak, but once he found his voice again, romance blossomed. As soon as Rhian heard Sonny speak, her heart belonged to him, and this was reciprocated. Sonny was always the gentleman though, a lesson he'd learned from Alf. 'Respect the fairer sex at all times, my boy. When you find the right one, you'll know. Your very soul will tell you to pursue the lucky lady and make her yours, but remember respect will always win the day.'

Sonny's physique was lean and muscular, with a triangular upper body you'd expect from a superbly fit athlete. Despite only being seventeen, he looked a couple of years older; his dulled eyes accentuating a lifetime of misery and pain.

Alf wanted to make sure that the future was better for Sonny. He put his name down at the local boxing club to legitimise his grandson's burgeoning reputation, but continued to train him himself on top of the mountain, and the results were spectacular! Out of the fifteen competitive fights already under his belt, Sonny had dispatched thirteen opponents in the first two rounds, and the two that went the full three rounds were two years older than him, but still he was victorious.

Sonny had an uncanny ability to say when he was going to knock his opponent out. He would give them a good look over, almost studying them. He would watch their manner, gait, size and confidence, and would then confidently, but not arrogantly, predict when he would bring the fight to an end. Quite a few of Alf's friends and associates made hefty financial gains from this.

But Sonny was a fair man. After the fight he would always shake his opponent by the hand to make sure he was OK, something else drummed into him by his grandfather. 'Once combat is done, the guy in the opposite corner is your friend, not your enemy,' he would say.

Although there was talk of a full apprenticeship in the building trade, a career as a pugilist was looking like a distinct possibility for Sonny Wilton.

But the wheels of fate never run a smooth path.

*

Alf was deep in thought and it had nothing to do with Sonny's training. Byron Lewis, one of Alf's more senior and influential working men, had asked for a meet, with Alf agreeing to see him at the mountain gym.

Byron was a nasty piece of work. He was over six feet tall, very muscular due to heavy weight work and steroid injections. And despite Alf's doggedness, was up to his eyeballs in drug dealing. Alf knew he was probably planning to take over the business, so he asked Kelvin, Myron and a few other trusted friends to come along. This proved to be a good tactical move; when Byron showed up, he was accompanied by half a dozen nasty looking heavies.

Alf was seriously considering retirement. If it wasn't drugs or weapons, it was brothels filled with east European girls, who had been promised a Great British life of milk and honey, only to be sold into a life of prostitution. He also believed that he owed Beth the final years of his life. Together, at their secluded Italian villa, they would finally enjoy peace and quiet – growing grapes and enjoying the warm climate, and Beth would no longer need to always be ready with an alibi, not that she ever complained.

And, of course, there was Sonny to consider too. Alf did not want him to join the family business. He was better than that. He was a contender!

'Morning, Byron. What kind of dirty fucking business brings you up the mountain at this time of day?' It was common knowledge that Byron Lewis and his crowd were night owls, selling drugs all over south Wales when the sun went down.

Byron offered a cold and insulting smile, but Alf knew that Byron was actually controlling the urge to punch him. 'Morning, Alf,' Byron said, smiling at Alf's friends as well.

One of Byron's cronies walked behind Alf like a gorilla and climbed through the ropes into Alf's makeshift ring. He looked at Sonny like a man would look at a misbehaving dog. Sonny, in return, leaned up against the ropes sizing up this flabby intruder. Sonny's face was void of emotion, even though Alf suspected his grandson was quite scared.

'I ain't gonna fucking beat round the bush, Alf. There's a lot of wedge to be made, and me and the boys want to reel some in.' Alf offered him a stern stare, a 'get the fuck out of my ring' kind of stare.

'We'd rather do it with your weight behind us, but to be

honest—' Byron looked defiant, cocky even, but Alf's stare had unsettled him, a bit.

Alf knew Byron would regain his confidence soon, so decided to tread lightly. He chose his words very carefully. 'Well you've got some balls, young Byron, the bollocks of an elephant I'd say. What's this all about? What would you rather do with my weight behind you?'

'Ecstasy pills, Alf. Half a fucking million of them.' Byron looked excited, like a child opening his presents on Christmas Day. 'There's a contact in Amsterdam, you see. He'll give us the first half million pills on tick. Should have cost us hundred grand mind.'

Byron moved closer to Alf and lowered his voice. 'Alf, these tabs are going for anything up to twelve quid a pop. The kids at the clubs and raves are chucking them down like fucking sweets. I mean, you do the fucking maths! There's scope to make us a bloody fortune, especially if we can make them ourselves. That's where you come in. I'm sure you can get the chemicals and equipment we need. We could be making our own in no fucking time at all. Come on, Alf, you've got to admit this is a winner. If we don't do it now, some other bastard will, and I don't want that to happen. No. Fucking. Way.' Byron waved his finger to emphasis the last three words, and then folded his arms in obvious defiance.

Alf's face gave nothing away. He looked the epitome of calm, but inside he was raging, fuming even. He controlled his natural urge to smack this bullying waste of space; to give this fucking bastard the beating he deserved. Instead, he moved in close to Byron, their noses almost touching, and looked directly into his eyes. He kept his voice calm and measured. 'This is my fucking business and I make the decisions. My *fucking* business. Not yours! I was doing this while you were shitting in your nappies, while your mam was wiping your snotty nose, while you and your brother were getting your bullying little arses through school. I took you on because no employer would. Don't you fuck around with me! You know I don't have any dealings with drugs.'

Alf stepped away from Byron, but still looked directly at him. Byron stared back with a cold hatred. Alf continued. 'There you have it, young Byron, the answer is no. Not in my name, ever. Not while I'm still drawing breath. If I hear of my name being connected to drugs, pills, powders, smoke or any other shit, you WILL face the consequences. Now get the fuck off my mountain, we're in the middle of a gym session.'

Alf turned and walked towards Sonny who was now shadow boxing to keep warm.

'Mr Wilton,' screamed Byron, in obvious discontent. Alf turned to look at the young pretender, and even though his pride was telling him otherwise, he was a little intimidated by the arrogance of Byron Lewis. 'I have always respected you, Mr Wilton, and everything you have done for me and my family, but times have moved on, sir, and we must move with them. I reckon you're making a big mistake, but we live and die by our mistakes, so I respect your decision. May I say, sir, your grandson is looking a fine prospect for the future.'

Byron then glanced over to the boxing ring and gave a nod to the big nasty looking thug who stood in the ring with Sonny. Everybody turned to watch as the big man launched himself at the youngster.

Sonny, who was more than expecting it, slipped the haymaker aimed at him with ease, and as the big man was forced forward by the momentum of his mis-timed punch, Sonny leaned down to his left, and let loose two rapid uppercuts right underneath his rib cage. The gorilla was beaten right there, but he bounced into the ropes and Sonny let fly with two hooks, left and right, either side of his ugly head, and the thug dropped to the floor like a dumped potato sack.

Sonny instinctively retreated to the corner of the ring, his guard up ready for another assault should it come, but he needn't have worried because the gorilla was on his hands and knees retching his guts up. Sonny dropped his guard and looked over to his grandfather with a questioning face, as if asking, 'Was that supposed to happen?' Alf gave Sonny a reassuring nod.

Inside, Alf was breathing a huge sigh of relief. Sonny had not only come out unscathed, but had inflicted a swift and severe beating to the bigger man. He turned to his antagoniser with a view to kill him there and then, but stopped himself with a calm that even surprised him. 'Drag that fat fucking ponce out of my gym and get the fuck away from me before I take care of the lot of you.'

Alf watched as Byron submissively gave the nod to his men, who in turn walked over to the ring to help the beaten man out. As they wrapped him around their shoulders, he was still struggling for breath.

Myron and Kelvin stood side by side with Alf, united.

Byron then let out a deep breath through pursed lips, and turned to retreat, but then turned back again. 'Like I said, I have always respected you, Mr Wilton, always have, always will, and you can't blame a bloke for trying to better himself can you? Very sorry for troubling you this morning, you have a good day.'

And with that Byron headed for the mountain path, followed closely by the thugs. Once they could no longer be seen Byron stopped dead in his tracks. He spun around and launched a brutal attack on the thug, who had already received a sound beating in the ring. He headbutted him and broke his nose. As he fell to the floor, blood oozing into his hands, Byron set about kicking and stamping on him. 'You big, fat, useless fucker,' he shouted, until the thug was unconscious.

Byron ran his fingers through his hair and, still breathing heavily, he looked to his right-hand man and best friend, Pete Sawyer.

'I've done my best with that old fucker, Pete. Agreed?'

His friend nodded calmly. He had grown up with Byron, done everything together: lit fires, broken windows and bunked off school. Nobody could pick a fight with one and not the other, they came as a pair – a damn formidable pair.

'Right then, Alfie boy, if it isn't the commonsense approach, we shall resort to other methods.' He looked into the eyes of all the other six men there; excluding Sawyer (his loyalty was unquestioned). The decision had been made.

'Right, we'll have one shot at this, so we'll have to bide our time, do our homework. This will not happen overnight, so not a fucking word outside the chosen circle. Is that understood?'

They all nodded, but even Byron was a bit nervous of the madness that was about to unfold.

'Right, pick up that useless fat cunt and let's get off this fucking mountain and back to civilisation. I could murder a cooked breccy. What about you, Pete?'

Sawyer nodded, although he was amazed at his friend's ability to talk food after announcing that he planned to take down the Wilton dynasty, but as usual he smiled and nodded in agreement. 'Mountain air builds your appetite.'

Byron retorted, 'Mountain air, my arse. It's 'cos I was riding that Paula all fucking night, and teaching that useless prick a lesson. I need to build my energy levels back up.' Smiling at his best and most trusted friend, he nodded to the severely beaten thug, who was now coughing up a serious amount of blood. 'Better dump him outside casualty.'

Byron strode purposefully down the mountain track. He was quite looking forward to the mayhem that he was about to unleash.

'Alf Wilton will rest in fucking peace, or even in pieces, once I've had my fucking way. And I *will* be having it my fucking way, rest assured.' That left him with one final decision. Whether to have tomatoes or beans with his cooked breakfast.

CHAPTER SIX
Getting Out

The Wilton kitchen was a nice, warm and homely place to be at most times. It was everyone's favourite room in the house, with the big farmhouse table in the middle. Beth always seemed to be pottering around cooking, baking or boiling the kettle for the never-ending tea or coffee on offer. As the years passed, Beth became the perfect and totally professional hostess. A lot of business, legitimate and otherwise, had been conducted in the kitchen. Alf always tried to shield Beth from the actual activities of the business, even though she would have done anything that he asked of her, but Beth also wanted Alf to retire. She ached to be somewhere warm, without the constant worries that the business brought.

Beth watched from her favourite armchair as Alf poured out three glasses of good quality single malt. As usual, Myron and Kelvin were keeping him company. Sonny was there too, on top of the work top, but he was not drinking.

It had been three months since Byron's altercation at the mountain gym, and Alf had noticed an uneasy atmosphere with business dealings since. For the first time ever, Alf didn't know who he could trust. This had sent him a clear message… The period of waiting was over, and the time for flight was now.

He had spent ninety minutes detailing his plans for himself and Beth and his two best friends. Things had to be done quietly and quickly. Finances had to be put in order, collected and distributed into various and easily accessible accounts. Alf had hidden away a great deal of money in a variety of places, but money never was his master. It was the business that drove him on, but from tomorrow his wife was going to be making sporadic trips into the city to start gathering that fortune into four easy access accounts.

Myron had never married and had amassed more than enough for his planned trip to Australia, where he had a brother who had been nagging him for years to make the move.

'I can't say I'm sorry to be packing it all in to be honest, Alfie. All the good days of us against the establishment and looking after our own have long gone. People like Lewis just want to turn over everybody for personal gain, but what about the people his drugs leave behind? I'm sick of it all to be honest. I'm ready to get out.'

All three men nodded in agreement at these heartfelt words; the drugs business and prostitution was turning the whole business ugly. It was a horrible, degrading vicious circle, with young girls getting hooked on drugs, having no choice but to let themselves be pimped out, just so they could pay for their habit. Added to this was the theft and burglaries to pay for drugs. The whole thing was rotting from the inside. Where had the traditional values of loyalty gone? Business was no longer done face-to-face, with a shake of hands, but with these new mobile phones and text messaging.

Beth had talked Alf into getting a mobile phone for emergencies, but this became another piece of clutter in his glove compartment, and the phone never worked anyway. Most of the time he couldn't get hold of anyone, or was cut off mid-conversation due to poor reception, but he knew how things were going. He was a dinosaur. Kelvin had been married as long as Alf. He had never let his daughters join any of the Wilton business activities. Instead they opted for legitimate jobs, got married and left home. Kelvin planned to buy a small place in Portugal, so he could disappear with his wife but be close enough if his family wanted to visit.

As for the Wilton trio, Alf had bought a villa with a small vineyard in the north of Italy. Nobody but himself, Beth and Sonny knew of its existence. He'd bought it many years before and the deeds were safely locked away in a solicitor's office in Cardiff. The plan was for them all to disappear on the same day.

Alf poured himself and his two friends another large whiskey. 'Remember though, don't tell anyone. As long as they know I'm still in charge we can get this done quickly and quietly.' Alf's two friends nodded their understanding, finished off their drinks and got up to leave. The three embraced and Alf let them out the back door.

Alf went to the armchair and stood in front of Beth, leaning down he put his hands on her shoulders, kissing the top of her head. 'You make a start tomorrow, my darling. Get the train to Cardiff. Go to all the companies on the list and they will know the drill. As far as those treacherous snakes are concerned, I'm going to Swansea tomorrow to buy another night club. I should be home around ten.'

Turning to his grandson, he raised both his hands in

mock supplication. 'Carry on as normal, Son, everything is the same. Go for your run. Hit the gym. Meet up with your mates. Keep everything the same, OK.' He smiled at the boy he loved dearly, almost as much as his wife did, if that was at all possible. 'Remember if it all goes wrong, it'll happen quickly. Don't be a hero. They won't hesitate in taking you down. Get to the stash and go. Do you understand, Son?'

Sonny nodded apprehensively. His stash was twenty thousand in used notes, alongside copies of his ID and contact number in Birmingham. This was sealed in a large water proof plastic container and was buried under the big log at the mountain gym. He could use one of the boxing ring posts to move the log, get the container and run. Sonny seriously hoped that things wouldn't come to that.

Beth, on the other hand, was elated. She had been hoping and praying that Alf would be looking for a way out, and now it was really happening – a legitimate life in Italy with their grandson. No more worrying about every knock on the door, or lying awake waiting for her husband to come home.

The next morning came with glorious sunshine. As Beth breezed around the house, no one would have suspected the threat of impending doom on the Wilton dynasty. Beth checked herself in the hallway mirror and went out of the front door, all smiles and happiness. Happy in the knowledge that a safe and contended life was, at last, getting close. She decided to walk the mile and a bit into town, instead of catching the bus or getting a taxi, then would get the train into the city. It was a lovely day, why not?

CHAPTER SEVEN
Falling Apart

Kelvin didn't know much about it when he got taken. He thought that as long as he heeded Alf's words he would be OK. His wife had been thoroughly briefed on what to do should he go missing. She was to collect their nest egg and go to their Anglesey holiday cottage and wait for news. If the news was bad, she would at least have a roof over her head, and would be safe.

Kelvin went about the next day pretty much as any other. He had a few debts, rent and protection money to collect, and that all went by without a hitch. He dropped the cash off at the Wilton's scrap yard office, and went off to *The Miners* for a couple, before he went home.

As a habitual loner, Kelvin was often left alone in the pub. He liked to sit at the end of the bar facing the door, with his trusty leather cosh tucked in his waistband. If anything was going to happen, he was always more than ready – but on this occasion the bar was unusually empty for the time of day.

Just before 9.00pm, the flimsy aluminium door burst open, its hinges snapping and glass shattering as it crashed to the floor. Kelvin, whose reputation as an incredibly tough man was no myth, was dragged away by eight of Byron

Lewis' henchmen. Like a pack of wolves, they were in for the kill, leaving Kelvin little time to reach for his cosh. He was bludgeoned to the floor as the henchmen kicked and punched him. One picked up a heavy bar stool and swung it down across Kelvin's knees three or four times, shattering them completely. Kelvin screamed! A smack across the head with a rounder's bat was unnecessary, but still they did it. Kelvin passed out.

The henchmen dragged him up, through the smashed doorway, and threw him unceremoniously into the back of an unlicensed Transit van.

Myron spent the day making sure his financial and legal documentation was in order. Over the years he'd been a shrewd investor, and now had a healthy cash flow that would last him over a hundred years, should he live that long.

As he sat back in his old armchair, Myron lit a cigarette and laughed gently. His gamekeeper's cottage hadn't changed much for the thirty years he had owned it. He was too selfish to get married – or have children – and would have probably been murder to live with. With a few steady girlfriends under his belt, and fast approaching sixty, it was probably a bit late to think about finding a Mrs Vincent.

He laughed again, took one last drag on his smoke, and stubbed it out in the chair ashtray. He had already decided not to tell his brother, Stephen, about his plans to permanently visit him in Sydney, instead planning to just show up on his doorstep, suitcase in hand.

Stephen had lost his wife, Sharon, to cancer two years back and, without any children to support, he'd welcome Myron with open arms. *The boys back together,* Myron thought, as he examined an old photo of his brother.

Suddenly all hell broke loose as Myron's door was ripped off its hinges by a sudden single blow of a sledge hammer. Four huge men in boiler suits and balaclavas emerged. This was not good!

Myron attempted to grab his old World War II pistol, but stood no chance; the four burly thugs were on him in a split second.

He grabbed his favourite glass ashtray and smashed it into the face of the nearest thug, cracking the man's cheekbone. The man screamed in agony.

Another thug grabbed Myron's hand and whacked a baseball bat down hard on it, breaking three of his fingers. The astray slipped out of Myron's hand. For a second time the bat made contact with Myron's wrist. A third sickening blow shattered his elbow and his arm fell to his side, completely broken.

Myron was then manhandled to his knees. A man, who appeared to be the ringleader, forced his head back, and with a knuckle duster repeatedly punched Myron in the face, his nose and jaw taking at least a dozen blows. Myron almost felt like he was floating, but when they let him go he dropped to the floor with such power that it dislocated one of his eye sockets.

Gaffer tape was wound around his head at least half a dozen times, sealing his mouth shut, followed by a hood to block out the light. His hands were then bound behind his back, and his feet were tied together.

As the thugs dragged him out, his head bounced repeatedly on the door steps. Just like a corpse in a body bag, they tossed him into the back of a van. The doors slammed shut behind him. Inside, Myron heard groans coming from the darkness. It was his lifelong friend, Kelvin. He was also in a great deal of pain! Before he passed out, Myron recognised Byron Lewis's right hand man, Pete Sawyer, barking orders to the henchmen. 'Straight to the fucking harbour,' he said. 'The boat is waiting and Byron's there as well, so don't fuck about. Go!'

Beth had carried out Alf's instructions to the letter. Most of the contacts on the list were pleased to see her. One or two were quite resentful when she asked to withdraw obscenely large sums of money. Beth was not normally suspicious, but she had the feeling that they had already been spoken to by someone else. She was only half way down that list when she decided to continue the job tomorrow. It was now getting close to 6.00pm and she had to run one or two personal errands.

The train home was packed with commuters. It was quite dark when she left the station and started the walk back to the house. She was halfway there when she stopped to look up the mountain, and at the house she had spent all her married life in. She had always loved her house, with its beautiful view from the living room down into the valley. She would definitely miss it.

She heard the Land Rover before she could see it. Its powerful engine was high revving as the driver tried to go as fast as possible. Beth turned to look as it came hurtling up the lane. She noticed that it had no registration plate. Worse still, the occupants appeared to be wearing balaclavas. A feeling of dread immobilised her for a moment.

She didn't drop her shopping bags or try to run, but just stood there, watching as her life came to an end.

The Land Rover smashed into Beth as the driver kept his foot on the accelerator and then reversed over her lifeless body. Her coat got caught up underneath the vehicle and she was dragged thirty metres down the road, before her tiny mutilated frame became untangled. The driver didn't even stop or slow down to make sure the job was done.

The little fishing boat had been a purchase that Byron was more than pleased with. The gang even used it as a proper fishing vessel now and again so as not to raise any suspicion, but its main purpose was to transport drugs and cash between Ireland and the coast of France. Alf would have stamped all over this enterprise, but Byron with his; 'Couldn't give a fuck' philosophy went ahead and bought the boat anyway.

Tonight the fishing boat, as it quietly made its way out to sea, was being used for something quite sinister. Kelvin and Myron were chained together on deck, with two hundred kilos of barbell weights threaded through the chains. Both had been severely beaten and were drifting in and out of consciousness.

After almost two hours the order was given to cut the engine. Byron stood at the front of the boat smoking a joint and surveying the scene before him. The darkness was all encompassing and added to the sinister atmosphere. He waved a loaded revolver around with glee. This made Pete Sawyer and the other six crew members extremely nervous, especially as Byron had been snorting cocaine all day.

Pete was not too pleased at being out late. He was on for a night's entertainment with an old friend and a couple of lovelies in Newport, so having to cancel really pissed him off. It didn't really bother him what was about to happen. He was more concerned that Alf had shown Byron the door. Nobody did this to Byron. They had it coming. They should have seen it coming.

Byron took a huge blast on the joint and flicked it into the treacle-like sea. 'You old fuckers have been taking me for an idiot for too fucking long,' he announced, leaning in close to the two trussed up figures. 'And you've left me with no bloody choice but to take matters into my own hands. You lot with your old fashioned 'no drugs bollocks' was quite frankly doing my fucking nut in.' He lunged forward and kicked Kelvin in the head.

'And so the grim reaper… That's *me* by the way… has called for a transition of power. Wilton will be dead by tomorrow night. His old lady is already fucking roadkill, and the little tough fighter bastard will be at the bottom of a derelict pit shaft as soon as we fucking find him.'

His eyes bulged with insanity as the six nervous but compliant gang members listened. 'I'm the fucking man now. What I say… what I do… and what I want done, fucking happens, got it?' Each man nodded. 'Get this pair up, it's time.'

Byron moved up close to the two hooded men and spoke quietly, 'I could be a real sadistic bastard and throw you to the fish while you're still alive, but not even I'm that fucking mental. I just want you to know that this isn't personal. Your wives and families will not be touched. I'll take an educated guess that you have set them up with a pension and a nice little bungalow somewhere safe and away from my business.

But they had better keep their ugly old mouths shut or I will find them, and they will be joining you.'

He then put two bullets each into the heads of Myron and Kelvin and the crew hauled their bodies over the side of the boat.

CHAPTER EIGHT
The Aftermath

Alf walked away from the mortuary after identifying his wife, his mind not of this world. Everything that was dear and precious to him had been taken away. He wasn't even allowed to identify Beth properly. Instead, he was given some of her belongings and shown a photograph of the birthmark on her shoulder. 'It would be too distressing for you to see her, sir,' they had said.

Alf had returned just after ten the night before. He had spent the day securing investment repayments in excess of two million pounds. He was cautiously feeling confident, but when he arrived home things were eerily quiet.

He had spotted two police officers waiting in a squad car outside his house, but thought nothing of this. Alf's dealings with the police over the years had been amicable. They did their job. He did his. Mostly, the authorities respected Alf for his iron grip on the crime figures in the district. As long as he wasn't an embarrassment to the local legal authorities, they pretty much left him alone. There were, of course, more than one or two senior officers that received an occasional Christmas hamper, with a nice fat envelope, that helped with the police pension fund or kid's school fees. Alf did his best to not take advantage of those contacts, unless there were desperate, unavoidable circumstances.

Alf had not been able to reach either Kelvin or Myron all day and this worried him. Despite having the mobile that Beth had talked him into getting, he still made a number of stops at pay phones during the day. He had called his friend's home phones, the scrapyard and even a few of the pubs, but no one had seen either of them, or they just weren't saying if they had.

He parked his car opposite the police vehicle, leaving the engine running and the door wide open. The constable sitting in the driver's seat appeared to look anxious. A sick feeling rose in his stomach. Something bad must have happened! Alf's mouth felt like it was full of sand, and a cold sweat crept over his body.

Alf knew the sergeant in the passenger seat. They had been in school together and, for a copper, he was all right. The sergeant walked towards him, and even though he was just crossing the road it felt like a lifetime. Alf opened his mouth, but said nothing. The sergeant reached into Alf's car and turned off the engine and took the keys out of the ignition. Then taking Alf by the arm, he steadily guided him to the front door of the house.

Once inside the house Alf sat down on his favourite armchair.

'I'm afraid I have some bad news,' said the sergeant, sitting on the sofa opposite.

Alf stared blankly at the police officer. He knew what was coming, but he didn't want to hear it.

'I'm afraid Beth was killed in a hit and run accident earlier today.'

Alf remained quiet for a few minutes, and then he snapped. 'Who the fuck did this? I'll kill the filthy bastard!'

'Please, Mr Wilton. Alf. We're looking into it. Let us do our job. We do know that a four by four vehicle was involved, but we're not certain of any other details at this stage. Can you please accompany us so we can eliminate you from our enquires, and you can make an identification?'

Alf's head was full of anguish as he walked away from the mortuary. Not being able to identify his wife's body made him openly brake down. He couldn't hold Beth's hand for the last time, stroke her hair, or tell her how sorry he was. That bastard had stolen these final moments. He would pay for this.

Later, Alf returned to the empty house and, once again, sank into his favourite armchair. Sonny was still not home. Had he got away? Did anyone warn him? Did he manage to get to the emergency stash and get away? His own world had just come crashing down, but now his mind raced to his grandson.

Alf knew for sure that Byron had murdered Beth. There wasn't much doubt about this. Myron and Kelvin had probably been killed as well. Alf knew it was time to disappear, but without Beth, life would not be worth living. He had never been a religious man, but he whispered a silent prayer for his lovely wife and his two best friends. He said another prayer for his grandson.

Alf didn't leave the armchair all night. He sat and wept until the early hours when, at last, he slipped into a restless sleep.

When he awoke the whole world seemed surreal, like a bad dream. The bastard better come for him soon. He had never been the suicide type, but he didn't feel as if his heart could hold out much longer.

He heard a noise. Was it a shotgun? *Sonny*, he thought.

Cautiously he unlocked the back door and slowly walked along the mountain path. He had run the three miles up this path thousands of times, but it never felt as long or as hard as it did today. Was Sonny hiding somewhere? And if he was, how was he going to get word to him? He broke into a jog for the last mile, and when he reached the gym, he ran straight to the log and dropped to his knees. There was the ring post and the trowel. The hole looked fresh and the soil was still dark and damp. The plastic tub was no longer there. *Sonny must have taken it*, he thought. He punched the air and then filled in the hole, burying the trowel. He moved the log back into place. He didn't want someone to discover the hole and realise that Sonny was safe. As he tightened the ring post back in place, he realised that he wasn't alone on the mountain.

Alf counted seven of them altogether, including Byron. He instantly recognised the big gorilla that had taken on Sonny in the ring previously. He didn't recognise any of the others, but guessed that they were employed by Byron. They all came to a stop about ten yards from the ring, except Byron, who kept on walking. He smiled at Alf who was now in the centre of the ring, staring back at his tormentor.

'You could've taken over in time, Byron. You didn't have to do it this way. You didn't have to kill my wife.' Byron's smile dropped and he looked at Alf with hate and disdain. 'Ah, but I wanted to see you broken, before I took it all from you. See, Alf, you've been making me look like a right fucking idiot for years now. It's been chewing my guts out, and I wanted…

No, I was absolutely determined to make sure that you lost everything. *Everything!* Before I took you down.'

Alf did not show any emotion.

'I also needed to demonstrate that I am the real deal. I don't want another fucker taking my prize. I took down Alf. The legend. Now I'm the fucking legend!'

Alf smiled. 'You'll be knocked off your fucking perch before too long. Someone will come for you and everyone will betray you. Mark my words!'

Byron stared at the older man in the ring and, without warning, pulled a pistol from his jacket pocket, and shot Alf in the face.

His body was dropped into an old coal board pit shaft and the very next day one hundred tons of concrete was poured into the shaft to make it safe from coal thieves, children and explorers. Some might say it was fitting that the king of the coal was buried in a coal mine. But not the way that it came to be.

CHAPTER NINE
Escape

Byron had every member of his crew out looking for Sonny. They bullied, beat up and threatened everybody that knew him, but it seemed that Sonny Wilton had disappeared into thin air.

Byron was pissed off. He could do without dangerous loose ends.

Detective Steven Sharpe was being paid a substantial amount of money to turn a blind eye. He had told Byron, in no uncertain terms, that there was to be no loose ends – no come backs. As far as the law was concerned, Alf Wilton and his closest allies had left for a warmer climate to enjoy their retirement, and all concentration would now be focused on the new generation of drug dealers, racketeers, thieves and vicious thugs.

But, as far as DC Sharpe could make out, there was no code of respect with these criminals. They would betray their own mothers, or give up their closest friends, if it meant making a few quid. DC Sharpe was nearing retirement, and the five grand a month from Byron was topping up his secret stash nicely. Alongside his police pension, he would have a comfortable life when he chose to knock it all on the head, but nevertheless, the power transition had to be quick, total, and with as little attention as possible.

'Well, the little fucker will have to surface soon,' Byron hypothesized. 'He won't be able to take a shit within a radius of twenty miles without me smelling it.'

In truth, Byron was nervous of Sonny Wilton. He heard whispers that some of the older crew members thought that Sonny Wilton was a chip off the old block, almost a clone of his grandfather. Byron was determined to put an end to this dissension, permanently.

As soon as Sonny got the message to run, he quickly contacted Rhian, who'd heard about Sonny's grandmother's untimely death. Sonny could see that Rhian had been crying.

'I need to go away,' he said.

'Where,' she asked, almost crying. She was expecting this news, but it was still a shock when he said it.

'Birmingham. One of my grandfather's friends will put me up.'

'What about me. You can't just leave me—'

'As soon as I am safe I will send for you,' interrupted Sonny. 'Keep your head down. Don't say anything to anyone.'

They kissed and held each other for what seemed like an age, and then he left her alone and heartbroken.

To begin with Sonny laid low in an allotment shed, just outside the village. He didn't sleep for a single second; his head was swimming with grief, worry and furious anger. Once he felt reasonably safe, he made the eight mile journey to the boxing ring, jogging nearly all the way. He was careful not to take any risks. Rather than follow his usual route, he zigzagged his way to the top of the mountain.

Thankfully, no one was there when he arrived. He swiftly found the trowel his grandfather had hidden, took down one of the ring posts to use as a lever, and moved the log. The digging took no longer than five minutes, but to Sonny it felt like an age. Eventually he found the container his grandfather had spoken about so many times. Exhausted, he crawled under the apron of the ring to rest. In less than two minutes he had fallen asleep.

Suddenly he snapped awake, hearing his grandfather's voice from the ring right above him. He was just about to call out to him when he realised that his grandfather was talking to Byron. For a split second he thought about launching himself at the murderous thug, beating him to death with his bare hands, but Byron was holding a gun. Clenching his fists, he calmed his breathing down. There appeared to be at least six men with Byron. Sonny was outnumbered. He would have to wait this one out.

Sonny flinched as Byron pulled the trigger. The bastard had shot his grandfather! The thud, as his grandfather hit the canvass, sent him into a terrified paralysis. He began to shake uncontrollably, clasping his hands over his ears to block out the dying sounds of the man he had worshipped all his life. Despite the blood seeping through the canvas and onto his face, Sonny stayed quite still. The shock was all-consuming, but he'd been through this before, and knew the implications of moving. He would have to stay there until the body had been disposed of.

Byron tucked the pistol into his trousers and turned to one of his crew. His nonchalant voice totally belied what he had just done. 'Right get down to the house and call Pete. Tell him it's done. Then chuck the dead fucker down the pit. Shaft A. The coal board are sealing it off this week. That'll be the fucking end of that.' Byron rubbed his chin as if to make sure he hadn't forgotten anything. It suddenly came to him. 'Oh, and ask Pete if he's still on for tonight? Tell him we'll do a couple of lines, and then the pub.'

The trusted gang member nodded.

Byron turned towards the rest of the group, who were nervously waiting for direction. 'Sam, get the body bag and gaffer tape. And you two…' He paused for obvious affect. 'Bag him up and get him down to the house. I've arranged for a van to be there. Once you've got rid of the body, I want you to find that fucking Sonny Wilton.' He turned to walk away. 'You others come with me. We'll do another sweep of the gym downtown. Shake a few fuckers up and find out where the little twat is holed up.'

He pulled out a pack of Marlboro, lit one up and took a long pull. Taking a last look at his old boss lying on the canvas, he then turned and walked down the mountain path, his three accomplices following close behind.

The thugs dragged Alf's body unceremoniously from the boxing ring and onto a makeshift plastic body bag. The men stripped Alf and emptied lime all over his body. They then used almost four reels of industrial gaffer tape to mummify the corpse.

While Byron's henchmen set about their grisly work, Sonny seized the opportunity to slip out from under the boxing ring and into the bushes to hide. This was fortuitous, as the last thing the thugs did was soak the ring with petrol.

Sonny watched as the ring went up in flames. Being mostly wooden slats and canvas, the blaze didn't last long and, in no time at all, it had been reduced to smoke and ash; years of training, sparring and fighting, gone!

Sonny stayed frozen for what seemed like an age, digesting the horror.

Now he had to escape; get to a place of safety, gather his head and build his strength. He would run, of course, but only so he could come back and bring Byron, and everyone associated with him, down.

Sonny stuffed the plastic container into his rucksack and took the cross country route to safety. As he turned into country lane, a bus heading to Cardiff pulled into a nearby bus stop. Sonny jogged to the bus and quickly got on. Exhausted, he took a seat at the back, burying himself in the corner. This way he could see everyone that got on and off.

Sonny got off the bus one stop away from the train station, a precaution in case anyone was looking out for him there. Once he was satisfied the coast was clear, he went into the train station and bought a one way ticket to New Street Station, Birmingham.

Cautiously he edged his way along the platform. He purposely stood at the very end, so he could see all the entries and exits. There was only a fifteen-minute wait, but it felt like an eternity. Sonny was exhausted and wasn't sure if he could run anymore.

The train pulled in. Sonny waited a few minutes to make sure the coast was clear. He then made a dash for the nearest open train door, threw himself into a seat and hunkered down. The minutes that followed felt like hours, but once the train doors closed he breathed a sigh of relief. Slowly the train pulled out of the station.

Sonny was totally exhausted. He had been taking short power sleeps these last few days, but as he sat in the warmth and relative safety of the carriage, his fatigue began to kick in. He started to dream…

Sonny is back on the mountain. Grandad has the pads on and is putting Sonny through his shots and combinations. Myron and Kelvin are leaning against the ropes watching and giving him encouragement and tips.

Then Sonny is running back down the mountain to the little house. After catching his breath he walks down the path and through the back door. There is his beloved grandmother, flitting around the kitchen as always, preparing the next meal for her two gladiators, as she jokingly calls them.

Then they are sat at the family's favourite place around the kitchen table, Myron and Kelvin included. Eating and chatting, planning the days ahead.

The back door gets kicked open and, in slow motion, Byron bursts in with a pistol in his hand. He starts shooting everyone at the table, except Sonny, and he's laughing like a psychopathic murderer.

BAM! BAM! BAM! BAM!

It seems to go on forever.

When he's done, everyone is dead, lying in twisted grotesque positions.

Except for Sonny.

Sonny looks on in horror at the carnage in front of him. He looks at Byron Lewis, who is still laughing, and then…

BAM!

The jolt of the train as it stopped at New Street Station snapped Sonny awake. It took him a moment or two to get his head back together. As he made an attempt to rub the tiredness from his eyes, a growing rage, an uncontrollable fury sped through his body. His rucksack had gone! Panicking, he checked the floor and the other seats around him.

'No, No, No! Please, no. Please, no!'

CHAPTER TEN
On the Run

Sonny had slept through the stop at Bristol. Anybody could have taken the rucksack.

How could he report this to the railway police? What could he say to them? 'Excuse me, officer. Someone's nicked my rucksack containing twenty thousand pounds in used notes.' No, this was not a good idea at all – but what an incredible touch for the thieving bastard; they would wet themselves with joy when they opened the rucksack.

Sonny slumped down into his seat and buried his head in his hands. The obvious hopelessness of it all eventually brought on the tears that he had been bottling up, and he sobbed uncontrollably.

An old Jamaican guard, doing a sweep through the train, came into the carriage and, without offering as much as a word of comfort, ordered him off the train.

Sonny aimlessly walked toward the exit of the station with all the other travellers. All of them hustling and bustling to their destinations. Sonny had absolutely no idea what he was going to do. He had no money, no belongings and no contacts.

And if he made his way back to Wales, he was dead.

Sonny wandered around the city centre, racking his brains as to what to do next. He had no family and no money. Just a few coins would help. He could then call his best friend, Neale, or even Rhian to send him some cash. But send it where? He would be eighteen soon, so the Social Services wouldn't offer much help. Going to the Police was not an option, as he would have to tell them the whole story. He might be lucky and find a copper that wasn't bent, but he couldn't take the risk.

It was starting to get dark and cold. Sonny hadn't eaten anything all day and was tired. Ducking down an alley by the side of a huge pub, he huddled up against the wall between two wheelie bins. Everything was hopeless. He pulled his beanie from his coat pocket and slipped it on his head, zipped his jacket all the way, pulled his collar around his neck, and buried his hands deep in his pockets. He slipped into a cold, restless and tortured sleep.

His eyes snapped open at the sound of someone relieving themselves, snorting phlegm up his nose and spitting it against the wall on the other side of the wheelie bin. The man spotted him and, after zipping himself back up and securing his belt, came and stood in front of him. He gave him a poke with a shiny Timberland boot.

'Oi, junkie fucker, the fuck you doing hiding down 'ere?' He gave Sonny another prod with his boot, a bit harder this time though, prompting Sonny to stand up and look the man in the eye.

'You fucking eyeballing me, bruv?' Sonny could see the guy was Asian, baseball cap, baggy jeans. He could smell beer and cigarette breath. He wasn't exactly drunk, but was on his way there.

'I asked you, bruv, you fucking eyeballing me?' Shouting down the alley the guy summoned two of his mates. 'Yo, Kam, Steve. There's one of them begging, stinking junkies down 'ere eyeballing me!'

Another Asian joined the guy, followed by a white man hurrying up the alley. The white man had the hood of his jacket up, and the other Asian had trendy tram lines carved into his buzz cut. All three men appeared to be in their mid-twenties and were dressed in similar street gang-style clothes. They were looking for a brawl. Sonny made an attempt to walk away from the brewing confrontation, but was shoved back against the wall by the Asian who had discovered him.

'We're fucking sick of you junkie fuckers begging around the city just so you get high on cheap fucking vodka and your fucking heroin.' The Asian, Timberland, was warming to the role of tormentor now. He jabbed Sonny in the chest. His cohorts started to weigh in with their own comments. It was hoodie first. 'Yeah, man, I gotta get up early every fucking morning to do my graft in the warehouse, and you junkie fuckers just fucking sit around with ya dirty blankets and your scabby fucking dogs. Getting people to feel sorry for ya, and give ya cash, ya fucking wanker.'

Buzz cut was next. 'Yeah, bruv, get clean an' find a fucking job. Pay some taxes, bruv, innit?'

Timberland moved in close to Sonny's face and snarled. 'You still eyeballing me, bruv?' But despite being a question it felt more like a statement. 'I'm gonna fuck you up, bruv.'

Sonny made another move to get past the three men. Timberland tried to shove him back against the wall, as the three men surrounded Sonny, their arms open in a 'come on then' gesture.

Sonny knew that Timberland would throw first. Speed was going to be the key. He would need to unload the big hits as soon as the fight started, with maximum damage in the shortest space of time.

Before Timberland could even send the punch forward, Sonny dipped to the side and let go with three pounding left hooks, one to the belly full of beer, another to the chest and the hardest one to the nose. The punch to the belly made the Asian instantly sick. The one to the chest knocked the air out of his lungs, but the finisher was the broken nose. The pain was instant, and went straight to the eyes. For a few seconds Timberland could see nothing but a white light. All confidence and bravado had disappeared. His brain went into surrender and flight mode.

Timberland dropped straight to the floor, desperately trying to suck in some air, throwing up his last pint of beer and spitting blood. He wouldn't be getting up in a hurry. A technical knockout the professionals would call it.

This momentarily shocked the other two and they both looked at the young man in disbelief, and then outrage for their fallen comrade.

Hoodie was the first of the two to react. He rushed forward with fists raised, but Sonny could already see that the bravado was quickly diminishing.

Meanwhile, Buzzcut bounced around on his toes, arms swinging by his side Bruce Lee style, about to launch into a combination of punches and kicks, Hollywood, or Bollywood style.

Sonny squared up to Hoodie in a southpaw stance, left hand lead. He sent out five stinging jabs to the face, sending his head snapping back with each blow. Hoodie was shocked by the swiftness of the punches, and sent a big roundhouse right hand punch in reply. Sonny slipped the punch, sending the bigger man lurching forward and off balance.

Sonny then delivered a blow that would have normally got him a ticking off from a referee – a 'fighting cheat' taught to him by his grandfather.

As Hoodie fell forward, the side of his head was exposed. Sonny hit him with a hard-open palm slap, straight to the ear. Delivered with a boxing glove, a blow that hard will cause huge pain as the ear drum absorbs the hit and disorientates a fighter for a few seconds; the opponent can then get a few more legitimate punches in. Receiving a blow that hard from an ungloved hand causes unbearable pain. The open hand creates a vacuum as the ear absorbs the pressure from the slap. When the hand is drawn away the eardrum can burst, causing excruciating pain, total disorientation and loss of balance.

Hoodie let out a roar of pain as he fell to his knees. He tried to get to his feet, not to continue with the fight, but as a means of escape, but he fell straight back down careering forward head first into the wall. He stayed where he fell, curled up in a ball, moaning against the screaming pain in his head.

Sonny turned to face Buzzcut, who had momentarily stopped bouncing around as he watched another of his cohorts being dispatched. Timberland, in the meantime, had crawled a few yards down the lane and had propped himself up against the pub wall, sitting on the floor still spitting blood and tenderly nursing his broken nose.

Buzzcut started his Bruce Lee-style bouncing back and fore again, arms swinging by his side. The look of panic and uncertainty on his face was by now plainly obvious. Sonny decided to put an end to this immediately. As Buzzcut bounced forward Sonny committed another old boxing cheat. He bounced forward himself and stood heavily on Buzzcut's leading foot. For a split second the Asian man looked down in confusion and the right uppercut caught him square on the jaw, sending him crashing into the wheelie bin unconscious. The whole fight was over, in less than a minute, and Sonny hadn't spoken a single word.

He let his hands drop to his side. He took a good look at the three assailants and, satisfied that they wouldn't be up for any more violence, he relaxed his shoulders and took in a few deep breaths. He took a look at his hands, apart from some redness on the knuckles they were good, no cuts.

His next immediate thought was money. As he searched Buzzcut's baggy jeans for a wallet he heard the five or six slow handclaps coming from behind him, further back in the alley. He squinted into the darkness. There was a sharp security light high up on the wall and Sonny could only make out a black silhouette.

'Damn, that was impressive, son. Quick and, may I say, bloody ruthless. Where the hell did you learn to fight like that?' The stranger had an unmistakable Welsh accent. It had faded a lot, as if he had been away from Wales for many years, but the lilt was still there, undeniable.

'You can enter this alley from back there. I could see it was gonna kick off so stayed in the shadows, just in case you needed any help, but I tell you what, youngster, you had more than enough, much more than enough.'

He moved away from the light and Sonny was able to make the man out. Mid-forties, a rugged 'seen it, done it' face, with a neat five-inch scar across his left cheek, and a very natural strong build. He was wearing walking boots, cargo trousers, a black lightweight raincoat and a Tilley hat.

'But I wouldn't do what you're about to do if I was in your shoes right now.' He moved forward. Sonny stood up, debating whether to make a run for it. The stranger lifted his hands in friendly submission

'You see, up till this moment, it's a simple case of self defence. They picked a fight, you kicked their arses.'

He stepped closer until Sonny was about six feet away. 'Tomorrow morning, after they've licked their wounds, there won't be another word said. They'll be too bloody embarrassed to tell anyone.'

The stranger nodded to Buzzcut, who was still lying on his side, next to the upturned wheelie bin.

'But if you take their money it could be described as a violent robbery. They will say they were jumped from behind, and beaten up and robbed. And you, my young friend, would be in a whole world of shit.'

Sonny looked into the strangers eyes. 'Mister, I am so desperate you wouldn't believe. I have already landed in a whole world of shit these last few days, and through no fault of my own. I've got no money, no possessions, no one to turn to and nowhere to go.'

The stranger immediately noticed the strong Welsh accent. 'And from where in the land of my fathers have you come from, my young Welsh brother?'

Still not about to trust the stranger, Sonny kept it simple. 'Valleys, Mynydd Du.'

'Pembroke myself. Put into the care system when I was two days old,' the stranger replied. 'Left Wales when I joined the Army at sixteen. Apart from Hereford and the Brecon with the Army, I've never gone back to Wales. No family there, no friends there. No point.'

Sonny again looked the stranger in the eye. 'I've had no choice but to get out of Wales, just this morning in fact, but I will be going back. Sooner or later I'll go back!'

The stranger offered his hand. 'Alan, but you can call me Patch.'

Sonny took the man's hand and shook it slowly. 'Sonny, as in sunny day,' he said.

The stranger laughed. 'And that is something you're most definitely *not* having today. You look like you could do with a large fish supper and a mug of tea.'

Sonny nodded in total submission. 'Starving. I haven't eaten since yesterday.'

'Well, I suggest we get the hell out of this bloody alley before these three superheroes fancy their chances again.' He started off down the alley, away from the three beaten thugs and towards the main street.

Alan noticed Sonny pull his hat down to cover as much of his face as he could. This raised his curiosity. 'And if you like, you can tell me your story, or as much of it you want to tell me, how's that?'

They found an all-night truckers' café near the wholesale market and took a table in the corner. Patch went to the service hatch and ordered and paid for a large fish, chips and beans for Sonny. Nothing for himself though. He never could stomach junk food. And two large mugs of tea. They were served to him straight away by a rather exhausted looking and rotund Jamaican lady. It took her two trips to get the food and beverages to the table. Alan took off his hat, revealing a fresh buzz cut and unbuttoned his raincoat. He sat opposite Sonny, scooped a spoonful of sugar from the bowl and, while stirring the sugar into his mug, he watched the young man attack his meal.

'OK, my young Welsh compatriot. You certainly look like you are in dire need of some assistance, but before that assistance can be applied or denied, you're going to have to tell me why you are in your current predicament.'

Sonny stopped chewing his food and laid the knife and fork onto the plate. He looked seriously at the man sat in front of him. He knew absolutely nothing about this man, but his gut instinct told him to trust him. There was something about the man's face that echoed his current pain; something visceral, something violent.

Sonny found himself telling Patch the whole story; from the meeting in the kitchen with his grandparents, to his grandmother's death, the execution of his grandfather, and the theft of his rucksack.

He then found himself backtracking and telling Patch about Alf Wilton and who and what he was. What he represented. That, although he was the head of an organisation involved in illegal organised crime, he was a fair man. Not exactly a Robin Hood figure, but he would always offer help where it was needed. Being able to talk to someone, even a complete stranger such as Patch, felt almost like he was in therapy, but it also brought forward the fury and rage again; the determination to get justice for his family.

Patch sat and listened to Sonny unburden himself. He didn't comment or question. He didn't show any emotion at all, just a nod or a shake of the head, a stroke of his stubble occasionally. If Sonny asked him for a thought, comment or his opinion, he would shrug his shoulders, answer with a short closed reply and encourage the young man to carry on with his story.

But he never once took his eyes off the boy's face. If there was one thing that Special Forces had taught him was to watch the eyes, then you could tell if someone is lying or telling the truth; the mannerisms of the speaker, constantly looking away or unable to maintain eye contact; an over convincing tone in the voice, trying too desperately to make you believe them. Well, this young boy told no lies.

Alan went to the serving hatch to fetch two refills for them both. He sat down and hooked his hands behind his head and looked out of the window. It had taken Sonny nearly three hours to bare his soul.

'Bloody careless on the rucksack. You should have tied a strap to your wrist when taking a power nap. There's no getting that back now. Twenty grand for a quick bag swipe though. That's a result for some thieving bastard, hey.' He leaned forward unclasping his hands from behind his head and rested his arms on the table. He let out a deep breath through pursed lips. Sonny slumped in his chair with his hands in his lap and nodded ruefully at his own huge error.

Patch then made a decision, and got up from the table, 'Right, let's go.'

Sonny looked up at him, questioningly. 'Where?' he asked.

'My place is about a forty minute drive outside the city. I drive in every couple of months to pick up some legitimate and some not so legitimate supplies, of which you may or may not be told about later.' He swigged the last of his tea. 'In the meantime, we could both do with getting our heads down. We can talk some more after a good sleep.'

Just the thought of being able to sleep somewhere safe was more than appealing to Sonny, but he had to ask. 'Talk about what?'

Patch had already started to walk out of the café. He turned back to look at the young man. 'I'm going to help you. Help you learn, plan and execute. Come on.' He nodded to the café door. Sonny didn't know whether to feel relieved or scared, but this situation was better than a few hours ago. He got up and followed Patch out of the café.

'Why are you called Patch?' he asked, once they were outside and he had caught up with his Samaritan.

'Seen the film Scarface?' Patch asked, pointing to the scar on his cheek.

Sonny shook his head

'Well, there's an actor in it called Al Pacino, or in my case Alan Patchino, Alan being my first name.' He said with an emphasis on the 'Patch'. 'Hence the nickname, Patch. My surname is actually Lawrence, but to be honest, if I heard someone calling out the name Alan Lawrence I'd think they were calling someone else. You see, I've been Patch for so long, hah!'

'And what about the scar?' Sonny asked, genuinely interested.

'That's a story for another day.'

They walked about a half a mile; down a couple of side streets and into a small industrial estate, where Patch pointed at an old Land Rover Defender parked in the shadows. He unlocked it and got in the driver's side and leaned across to let Sonny in. The old diesel workhorse roared to life. He turned the heating on in the vehicle and drove off. That was enough for Sonny. He fell asleep and stayed that way until they reached Patch's place.

CHAPTER ELEVEN
Alan 'Patch' Lawrence

Alan Lawrence was put into the care system at two days old by an eighteen-year-old mother. After discovering that a worker from the travelling fairground had made her pregnant, her deeply religious parents had kept her locked up at home until the baby was born. They could not, and would not, live with the embarrassment of having a bastard baby under their roof. So, it was decided that the mother would surrender all rights and responsibilities, and the baby would be given the chance to have new parents.

Sadly, in Alan's case this was not to be; being one of the 'left' children that slipped through the system. Nobody seemed to want to take him – and when he had gone past the babe in arms stage, to a toddler, the chances of him finding a loving family were reduced even further.

He remained in care for all of his childhood. A normal family life, with parents and siblings, was alien to him. This made him a perfect candidate for the Army.

And he joined up at sixteen.

He took to army life like a duck to water and became a textbook and exemplary soldier. His fitness levels and attention to detail were second-to-none. At twenty one he applied, and was immediately accepted for Special Forces selection testing in the SAS.

He passed selection with flying colours, spending the next ten years of his military career as a sergeant in 20 SAS. He visited countries and conflicts all over the world, from Belfast to Belize.

He was asked to stand down from front line operations at the age of thirty-one. Instead, he became a trainer and instructor in survival – and armed and unarmed combat – for Special Forces recruiting.

While he was working in South Africa, sharing training methods and techniques with their own Special Forces equivalent, he met and fell in love with a black South African woman named Amara, whom he intended to marry.

The elders in her village were not happy with this for various colour, creed and juju reasons. One day, seven men from the village hacked her to death with machetes in the home where she lived by herself.

Sergeant Lawrence went berserk. He hunted down Amara's killers one by one, murdering each one with various, vicious and bloody methods.

He used all the tactics of stealth and cunning that he had learned through his years with the Special Forces. Although the Army knew that he was responsible for the killing of the seven Africans, he was never charged. Nevertheless, he was dishonourably discharged from the Army at the age of thirty-seven, after twenty-one years of service – fifteen of those years with the SAS.

He found himself in London working as a private bodyguard;

mostly for the extended members of the Saudi Royal Family and Saudi diplomats.

His last position was providing bodyguard protection for a very wealthy Saudi diplomat and his family. This included his wife, daughter and two sons. All was fine, apart from the daughter, who was a live cannon to say the least. Considering her tender age of sixteen and that she was from a country with deep religious beliefs, she was a true lover of the adventures to be found in London's night life. She could regularly be found at parties and clubs across the capital.

One night, she had ventured into a part of town where she had no business being – and was descended on by a group of Jamaican gangsters. They forcibly coaxed her out of a back door of the club – with the intention to gang rape her – when Lawrence, who had been shadowing her all night, came out of the darkness. Something hidden in the back of his mind brought back the memories of his beloved Amara, and he inflicted serious damage to the Jamaican gang.

The diplomat was obviously extremely grateful to Alan for not only saving his daughter's purity, but possibly her life. Being typically Arabic, the whole episode was hushed up. No attention or publicity was drawn to the family. This silence was absolutely paramount. Alan was knifed during the fight and, in the middle of the night, this injury was dealt with by a Harley Street surgeon, hence the very neat scar. The surgeon would, of course, ask no questions as long as his huge fee was paid. In cash.

The nickname 'Patch' was given to him by others in the security world, after receiving the wound and subsequent scar.

The diplomat and the family left London for good and headed back to Saudi Arabia two weeks later.

Before departing, he asked Alan to meet him privately in a city hotel room where he rewarded him with five hundred thousand pounds in used notes for his service and loyalty. Alan had to promise, in return, to never mention the incident with the daughter. He immediately agreed to this. The habit of keeping job or mission details to himself had been drilled into him from his Special Forces days.

Immediately, he decided to retire from the security business. He was forty-two years old and moved to central England.

A chance meeting with a farmer in a pub in Birmingham led to him becoming a gamekeeper on a farm outside the city. The farm owner sold him a large barn that stood on the outskirts of his land and Patch converted it up to a comfortable living standard, and although it still looked like a barn it suited Patch perfectly.

As well as the shotguns he kept for his gamekeeper's job, he became an expert with a crossbow. His survival, stealth and combat skills would always remain with him. That kind of expertise stays in the blood, forever.

His skills in shooting and trapping, and his ability to stalk and hunt prey for days, earned him a good reputation with the local farmers. Subsequently he became the gamekeeper for nearly all the farms in the surrounding area. Living in the countryside, and all the peace and quiet that came with it, suited Patch perfectly. After four years he was still very happy, and as far as he was concerned would be staying where he was, permanently.

CHAPTER TWELVE
The Barn

Sonny slept through most of the journey, but as Patch pulled off the road onto the long gravel lane, Sonny woke with a start. It was 4.00am. Sonny had no idea where he was, but he felt safe. Patch had promised to help him: to learn, plan and execute. This made little sense to Sonny, but he was grateful for the offer to help him.

Patch reached behind the passenger seat for his shopping. 'Time for some grub, I reckon.' Sonny nodded and opened the passenger door. It was a bit stiff; almost as if nobody used it much. Patch walked around the front of the vehicle and stood in front of Sonny. 'There's a saying,' he said, staring straight into Sonny's eyes. 'Revenge is a dish best served cold. Well, all I can say is bollocks to that.' He tossed his car keys into the air, almost dropping them, and then moved towards the barn. 'Cold means poor planning, poor preparation and poor execution. Revenge is a dish served red hot.'

Sonny nodded, trying not to blink.

'It's all about the ingredients: knowledge, training, planning, practice, and, most importantly, repetition. Every detail must be meticulously planned and repeated over and over, until success is guaranteed. Then you serve it up and ram it down their throat. The execution!'

Sonny almost gulped; he'd met some unsavoury people in his life; men that would betray their mother for a packet of fags, but Patch was different. He seemed cold and calculating. Sonny edged towards the barn, but Patch stopped him, with a firm hand to the chest.

'Stay there,' Patch said, his eyes signalling danger. Patch pushed open the barn door. There was a twang from the darkness and a 'swoosh' sound as a crossbow bolt came shooting through the doorway at knee height. It embedded itself in the trunk of an ash tree about fifteen feet away. 'The way I see it, if a burglar finds a solid and well-locked door his curiosity is raised. What's behind the door? What's worth nicking? The burglar is going to be quite determined to get in, isn't he? He could do all kinds of damage to my place. But if he finds an unlocked door and, in he goes, he's going to get the fucking shock of his life.'

Patch looked searchingly into Sonny's face. 'You and your family have been hugely wronged, and you are well within your right to want revenge. But right now, today. You are nowhere near prepared for it. You don't have the necessary skills or knowledge. Sure, you could acquire a gun, turn up somewhere blasting away, and quite possibly shoot them dead, but then you'll probably be locked up for God knows how long. Or these people will catch you before you've started, and you will disappear, just like your grandfather.'

He put a hand on Sonny's shoulder, almost like a parent would comfort a child.

'But if you are patient, and you look, you listen, and you learn, things will be different. There will be a plan. You will execute this plan. You will get revenge for your family. And then you will move on.'

He pushed open the barn door again and beckoned for Sonny to step inside. Sonny made a move, but then stopped dead. 'Y'know what, after you,' he said, with a playful smile.

Patch laughed. 'You're learning very quickly, my little Welsh brother. Come on in.'

Patch ventured into the darkness, flicking the switch that lit up the huge room. He took off his hat and coat and threw them on an old settee that was pushed up against a wall near the door.

Sonny inspected Patch's crossbow trap. It was ingenious. His grandfather would have been impressed. Sonny looked around the room. The barn was on two levels. The floor level was windowless, but well lit. It seemed to be fortified with heavy beams criss-crossing and bolted to the already solid wood walls. All kinds of gym equipment: free weights, dumbbells, barbells occupied the space. Sonny looked over at Patch who was putting away the shopping. Patch was no old soldier; he was built for strength and looked like he could jog for twenty miles, hunt down and kill a buffalo, chop down an oak tree to build a fire, and then eat said buffalo.

Much to Sonny's delight there were two heavy punchbags and half a dozen pairs of bag gloves scattered around them. There was also a pair of sparring pads and a heavy medicine ball.

Patch pointed towards the downstairs area. 'My classroom,' he said. There were two benches positioned in front of a large chalkboard. Stacked neatly against the chalkboard were some old munitions boxes, contents unknown. 'If this goes the way I expect, we'll be spending a great deal of time there.'

Patch walked to the middle of the room. Thrusting his hands into his trouser pockets he looked, almost quizzingly, at the young man before him. Truth be told, Patch could retrain or re-programme experienced war weary killers, mercenaries or soldiers with vast experiences of killing.

But this was new territory for him. Sonny, most definitely – desperately – needed his help, but apart from his excellent fighting skills, the lad possessed no other specialist skills. In his experience, men blinded by retribution usually armed themselves for the apocalypse, but often got themselves killed, long before they even reached their tormentor.

If this kid really wanted his help, and Patch's intuition was telling him that he did, Sonny would need to be patient. He would have his day, but it would take a lot of work. 'We'll start tomorrow,' he announced. 'I don't know about you, but it's a bit late for food. I need some shut eye. Come on.' He headed towards the staircase. Sonny followed, his head bowed.

At the top of the stairs was a large room with an equally large window. Its vertical blinds were closed, but the early morning light was starting to find its way through. In the centre of the room were four light brown leather three-seater settees, positioned in a square so they all faced each other. The solid wood floor was polished and had various quality mats and skins dotted around. A big comfortable looking armchair sat strategically in front of one of the windows, so it took in the best view of the surrounding countryside. A very large and heavily padlocked gun cabinet stood bolted to one wall. At one end of the room was a log burning fire, and four large bookcases, covering everything from historic military battles to urban survival.

In a corner was a small kitchen area, with a four-seater dining bench. Next to this was a large wet room. Patch had built two bedrooms, one in each corner. Obviously, one was for himself. He pointed to the other. 'That will be home for you for a while, make yourself comfortable. All the bedding you need is in a drawer under the bed. When any of my old army buddies come to stop I make sure they bring their military cot with them and sleep downstairs. So, no one has actually used that room as of yet, so you can consider yourself a privileged guest.' He walked Sonny to the room, reached in and turned on the light. 'You look not far off the same size as me, so I'll sort out some clothes and training gear for you tomorrow.'

Sonny looked at Patch. This total stranger was offering him shelter and help. 'Thank you so much, Patch. I promise I will work hard.'

Patch nodded in agreement. 'You're going to have to, kid. If you want to go back to Wales you need to be prepared. I can teach you, but you must have the patience and adaptability to learn.' He started to walk towards the kitchen area, then turned back and looked at Sonny very seriously. 'This man wants you dead and, as far as he's concerned, you *should* be dead. But thanks to the foresight of your grandfather, you're alive. This is going to piss him off immensely. If he gets another chance, he *will* go after you. He sees you as a threat. You *are* a threat. All we need to do is turn that threat into a mission of stealth, guile and vicious retribution. Now sleep. Tomorrow you will have your first lesson.'

Sonny closed the bedroom door and threw his beanie and jacket onto the bed. He walked over to the window and drew the curtain. A small sink stood in the corner with a mirror over it. He splashed some water on his face and stared at his tired and stressed features. His brain was still swimming with recent events, but now what?

He felt sure he could trust Patch. He believed that he would help him. But teach him? Teach him what? Sonny kicked off his trainers, pulled open the drawer and dragged out a very thick duvet. A sheet and two pillows were already neatly set up on the bed. He finished undressing and got under the sheets.

Yes, he knew he could trust this man. He fell into a deep and welcome sleep.

CHAPTER THIRTEEN
Student Again

Sonny snapped awake, after what seemed like a quick power nap. It was, in fact, just after midday. He had slept solidly for nearly seven hours. Climbing out from under the warm duvet, he opened the curtain to take in the nice sun-drenched afternoon in the countryside.

After a quick splash with cold water, he pulled on his dirty jeans and t-shirt and opened the door to the bedroom. Patch was sitting in the big armchair. He was wearing a black tracksuit and running shoes. He had been flicking through a huge book of survival and combat techniques. He closed the book with a snap, put it down on a small table to the side of the chair and turned to Sonny.

'Good morning… or I should say, afternoon? After yesterday's and this morning's adventures, I thought I'd let you catch up on some sleep. Tomorrow you will be up and ready by six fifteen, OK. Awake at six, and ready to go at six fifteen. Is that clear?'

Sonny nodded eagerly. Structure and direction is what he definitely needed right now. He was going to prove to be a willing and attentive student. 'Yes, sir,' he replied.

Patch smiled at the young man. 'No need for the "sir"

thing. Patch will do. There's a few tracksuits, t-shirts, gym kit, running shoes and outdoor gear on the sofa for you. We can pick up anything else when you need it. Now, breakfast! Will eggs and bacon do you?'

Sonny nodded appreciatively.

Patch moved into the kitchen. 'Well, come on then. Eggs and bacon won't cook itself,' Patch snapped, but in a friendly enough tone. Sonny moved sharply to the kitchen.

After scrambled eggs, bacon and toast, and a clean-up of the kitchen, Sonny picked up the pile of clothes and footwear donated to him by Patch. There was also a wash bag, with a toothbrush and toothpaste, a bar of non-fragrant soap, and a bottle of non-fragrant shower gel.

Sonny carried everything into the bedroom and, after cleaning his teeth and a quick wash, he changed out of his jeans and t-shirt into an olive green army issue tracksuit.

Patch then led the way down the staircase to what he referred to, and would from now on be known as, "the working area". He made his way to one of the two benches in front of the chalkboard and gestured Sonny to sit. Sonny did as he was told, but felt strangely nervous at the bizarre scenario.

Patch took a notebook, with a pencil wedged in the spring binder, from a shelf near to the chalkboard and sat himself opposite his new prospective protégé. He placed the notebook on the bench and pushed it towards Sonny. 'Apart from the fighting techniques I will teach you, I expect you to make notes on everything else that you are shown. You will then learn, practice, demonstrate and repeat. Learn, practice, demonstrate and repeat. Learn, practice, demonstrate and repeat. Do you understand?'

Sonny did not reply. He grabbed the notebook and removed the pencil. He opened it to the first page and wrote in capital letters, 'LEARN. PRACTICE. DEMONSTRATE. REPEAT. Once he had finished writing, he flipped the notebook shut, slid the pencil back into the binder, and he looked back at Patch and nodded. 'Yes.'

Patch smiled and nodded. *This boy is going to learn*, he thought. 'Today we are going to walk the path,' he said. 'It's a five mile circuit through the woods. You will run it every morning from now on. From what I've seen of your boxing skills, you should be well used to that kind of run. I don't expect to see you run it quicker as time goes on. I want to see you finish the run and recover your normal breathing within a minute, two at the most, after finishing. It's possible you might be on the run from someone, and you may have to stop, set a trap or even confront them, and fight it out.'

'If your breathing has recovered by the time they catch up, you have the advantage. You will be stronger. You attack then, quickly and viciously, while their breathing is still laboured. A nice thick bit of timber to the solar plexus or a rabbit punch to the Adam's apple. They will go down, trust me. The fight will have left them before it has even started.'

Sonny nodded at Patch's logic. He was certainly right about him running. For a few seconds he cast his mind back to the mountain gym back home. He used to run alone or with his grandfather – uphill all the way!

They left the barn, but this time Patch did not lock the door. 'We're not leaving the area,' he reasoned.

They walked away from the barn and into a wooded area, the path almost invisible. Patch quickly explained his gamekeeper's role for the surrounding farms, saying that usually he pleased himself, unless he got a phone call asking for his help with a pest fox or badger.

If he fancied shooting some rabbits, crows or a hare or two, he would set up a 'hide' where the pest had been making a nuisance, and stay there for days sometimes, usually until the human smell had gone. Normally, the animal will regain its confidence and show itself.

Patch most definitely didn't do it for the money. He didn't need the money. The farmers would drop him off a few quid here and there. He would always get fresh produce during the harvests and a whole lamb when the season was in, but that was it. With his enhanced army pension, and the money left from the five hundred grand, he was doing OK. And he did, of course, own the barn and the surrounding three acres outright.

Anyway, if the proverbial did hit the fan financially, there was still plenty of mercenary work. He was still fending away offers from war ravaged countries, and the skills he possessed would always be sought after.

After they had walked for about half a mile, Patch started his first survival lesson; finding food sources. Hunting wild animals is both time consuming and it can take years to develop the necessary skills and, more often than not, can attract unwanted attention. Traps and snares can give a limited amount of success.

Patch showed Sonny berries that were edible and white and yellow berries that were poisonous. He made him aware that fifty percent of red berries are poisonous. Single pieces of fruit hanging from a stem are usually safe to eat, but fruit divided into five sections is more than likely unsafe. He taught Sonny how to recognise either the bitter almond or peach smells, meaning that they are poisonous to eat. He showed Sonny what leaves are edible, such as dandelion and nettle; which ones should be eaten raw; and which ones needed to be boiled before eating. He showed him how to get short energy bursts from the inner bark of trees like Birch or Maple, or how to shell Oak acorns, boil them over, and then roast them before eating. Sonny also learned how you could turn boiled water into a stock, by adding primrose leaves and make the resulting soup quite tasty. Patch stopped after every quick lesson so Sonny could scribble short memos in his notebook. When they came across two particular plants, he instructed Sonny do some quick sketches and memorise them. These were Foxglove and Deadly Nightshade. 'Stay clear of these, unless you intend to use them as a weapon against your enemy. Even then, handle with gloves, especially Deadly Nightshade. It's fatal. Also, I have a lifelong dislike of mushrooms, so I just avoid at all costs. I advise you to do the same, too risky.'

Patch walked to the trunk of a huge Oak tree, picked a stick up and poked away at a toadstool.

'Amanita Phalloides, commonly known as the Death Cap. A short while after eating as little as half of one of these bad boys your whole world will exit through your arse… and you will develop uncontrollable vomiting. After a day or so, your liver will no longer function. The same applies to the kidneys. There is cranial pressure as the brain swells. Death can be within four to ten days, probably by heart failure.'

He looked up at Sonny. 'Mushrooms, if you really want someone to suffer.'

Sonny looked intrigued. He made a quick sketch, noting the mild green colour, and listed the deadly symptoms. He put the notebook back into the pocket and waited for the next lesson. His face held no expression. Patch was a little impressed.

'I want you to learn as much as you can about food sources – the good and the bad on offer to us by Mother Nature. Sometime in the future we will camp out here, with just a knife and appropriate clothing, and you will attempt to feed us both.'

Patch walked back along the path. 'I will teach you how to make an overnight hide, here in the countryside. I will then show you how to dismantle it in the morning, so nobody knows you've been there.'

He marched ahead a short distance, but carried on the lecture.

'I'm going to teach you how to watch someone's habits and daily routines for as long as it takes, until you can absolutely, confidently talk me through their plans. I will teach you how to walk freely around that home, business, warehouse, shop or anywhere else.'

Sonny's head looked like it was spinning. Patch had given him a reality check, but he wasn't done yet.

'You've got outstanding boxing skills, but you will also have to learn some dirty stuff: wrestling and grappling, killer punches, choke holds and kicks; how to pretend you're beaten; how to make noises and pretend you're hurt. It's called stealth and guile.' He walked back to Sonny and stood face to face. 'Your opponent will think he has you where he wants you. And he will let his guard down. Then you strike!'

Sonny licked his lips. 'I can do this. I need to do this. I

can learn, and once I've learned, I'll learn it again. You don't know me, Patch. Once I've set my mind to something, I won't let it go.'

Patch could tell that Sonny meant what he said. He knew that the young man genuinely wanted to learn. In all fairness, the boy seemed unfazed.

'Right, we've still got a few hours we can put in today. Let's run the rest of the five mile and we'll do a couple of hours in the barn.'

Sonny liked the sound of that and started to stretch his legs out. 'Lead the way then, Gaffer. After today you'll be coming second on the five mile.'

'Not with fourteen pounds of sand in a rucksack you won't, you cocky bugger,' Patch retorted back, and set off at a decent pace down the path.

'Oh shit.' Sonny muttered under his breath as he set off after his new trainer.

The three miles that were left to run felt like balm to Sonny. The last time he had been running in this kind of terrain was after his grandmother's hit and run. He'd felt terrified but today, to some degree, he felt safe again.

He was still in shock. His stomach lurched every time he thought about the last few days, but he was starting to come to terms with the fact that he was out of his depth and he needed help. For some unexplainable reason, he trusted Patch completely. He felt safe in his company, and truly believed him when he said that he was going to help him. So, he enjoyed the run.

CHAPTER FOURTEEN
The Class

It was just after four when they arrived at the barn. They both stumbled into the yard, with hands on their knees to recover their breathing. Patch returned to normal breathing first. Sonny wasn't far behind.

Patch unlocked the door. 'There's a shower in the working area. I'll use that one. You use the one upstairs. Meet at the chalkboard in fifteen minutes, OK.'

Sonny nodded and raced up the stairs, two at a time. He was in and out of the shower in less than five minutes, and was wondering what was coming next as he pulled on a grey t-shirt and matching tracksuit bottoms.

When he made his way back down to the working area, Patch was already standing in front of the chalkboard. He seemed to be swinging a set of Allen keys in one hand. One of the munitions boxes had been put on the bench. Sonny quickly sat down. Curiosity was eating him up.

'You may have seen these before,' said Patch, pointing at the Allen keys. 'But I am going to assume you haven't. These are lock picks.' He pulled the lid open on the munitions box. It was full of all kinds of locks. Front door locks, back door locks, mortice locks and padlocks. All kinds of makes, all kinds of styles, and all kinds of sizes.

For the next two hours Patch explained the intricacies and complexities of barrel and lever locks. He used the chalkboard to illustrate the inside of these locks, showing how the barrels or levers locked and unlocked. He also explained the weaknesses and failures of the locks.

'Sonny, what's the first rule of breaking and entering.' Sonny shook his head. He did not know. Despite his unconventional upbringing, he wasn't that practiced in burglary.

'To be honest, I'm glad you don't know. Anyway, the first rule is to get up close to the intended entry point. Take a good look and memorise the lock. Then go away and practice how you are going to spring that lock, without causing any damage. You can then break in when you are ready, but only when you are ready. Always leave the premises in the same secure condition that you found it. If there are any clues that the premises have been entered illegally you may as well have kicked the door down.'

Patch taught Sonny what use each 'pick' had, and how sometimes two picks or even three were used to spring the more intricate door locks. A vice had been mounted on a small bench to the side of the chalkboard, and Patch set up various door locks. One after the other he demonstrated how to open them. Dozens of padlocks were spread out; locked then unlocked; and then locked again. Other strange lock picking tools were demonstrated, especially if the conventional ones didn't do the trick. Sonny was certainly enthusiastic, but there would be no miracle start and, to his obvious annoyance, he didn't manage to open a single lock or padlock.

Patch reassured him that this was absolutely normal. He joked. 'If it was that easy to pick a lock, there wouldn't be a locked door in the country. What would be the point?' He put his hands on the table. 'It'll come you'll see. It's that word 'practice' again. Keep at it. *Every* day. No token gestures. Serious concentrated effort, and it'll happen. Once you've cracked this, we can start having some fun. It isn't all work, y'know.' He smiled at Sonny and got up from the bench. 'That'll do for today. Let's get something cooked up. I don't know about you, but I'm starving.'

After a hearty meal of stir-fried chicken, bell peppers and brown rice, they both sat down and Patch pressed Sonny more on the events of the last few days. It wasn't that he didn't believe or trust him. He just wanted him to unburden himself; a layman kind of therapy. God knows he had known men with post-traumatic stress disorder that had gone insane with the horror of the memories of bloody battles.

Sonny recalled the events once again and explained that he'd left his lifelong sweetheart, Rhian Hughes, in the line of fire. Patch could tell that they were obviously besotted with each other and warned that the situation could be dangerous for them both. This would need to be meticulously monitored, in case there was a need for a plan B.

Just before 9.00pm Patch could see that Sonny was flagging. He went over to one of the book cases and pulled out a book on hand to hand and unarmed combat from the Royal Marine Commandoes and offered it to Sonny. 'Bedtime reading,' he said. 'Go on, off you go.'

Sonny tucked the book under his arm and made his way to his bedroom. Before he shut the door, he looked over to the soldier who was carrying an empty cup over to the sink in the kitchen 'Thanks again, Patch.'

Patch didn't look back at Sonny. 'Long way to go yet, my young Welsh brother. Thank me when you're ready. Or better still, when it's all over.' He turned on the hot tap and swilled the cup clean.

Sonny switched on the bedside light and closed the bedroom door. He undressed and did his evening ablutions, then climbed into bed. He set the bedside alarm clock for 5.55am. He opened the book that Patch had given him to read, and had truly intended to make a start, but within seconds he was fast asleep.

The alarm was beeping loudly in the dark. *I must have turned the bedside light off sometime during the night*, he thought. His jeans that he had laid on the floor in front of the bedroom door – a trick that patch had taught him yesterday – were undisturbed, and exactly where he had positioned them last night. He was quickly out of bed and at the sink. He swilled his head with water and soon he was wide awake. He pulled on his tracksuit, slipped on and laced up his running trainers, and soon he was out the bedroom door. It was five past six in the morning.

Patch was already up and dressed. He looked out of the window next to the large armchair. 'Good morning. The time is five past six. I said to be up at six and to be ready at six fifteen. Timing Sonny, timing. The end result of being too early for a mission or a job can be just as catastrophic as being late.'

He walked over to the confused looking young man.

'You might have spent days, maybe weeks studying your target. You know exactly what time they come, what time they go. You've noted that they stop at the shop when they have left for work to pick up a newspaper. They stop at the same shop on their way home from work to pick up something for their evening meal. Timing, routine, habit. You know to the second, when you can enter their premises, whether it's to take them out or search for something you want, and how long you have till you must leave. You can't move too late. You can't move too early. Precision timing. In this case, I gave you a precise time. You were ten minutes early.'

'If that was a scenario where you were going to ambush or even kill someone, imagine if you were ten minutes early. You'd have to wait around, wouldn't you? What if you're seen and you're target gets tipped off, and he himself makes a few calls? Ten minutes is plenty of time to get a few thugs together and give you the fright of your life.'

Sonny looked sheepish and felt foolish at this schoolboy error. *Being early equals keen*, he thought. *No, being early can get you hurt or killed.*

He took out his notebook from the back pocket of his tracksuit bottoms. He flicked it open and wrote, 'Precision timing, precision habit, precision routine.' Underneath he wrote, 'Execute all work to the second. Never late. Never early.' He replaced the pencil and put the book back into his pocket.

'Got it,' he said.

Patch was pleased that Sonny had taken the mini-lecture in the serious context that it was meant, and that he had made a note in his book. This told Patch that the boy was listening and learning. Sonny could have got the hump. Instead he accepted that he had made an error. He was told an exact time to be ready. He was too early. In a different environment, the results could have been disastrous. Best to make these mistakes now and get them ironed out.

He raised a quick smile at Sonny, just to let him know that this particular lesson was done and nodded toward the kitchen work top. 'There's a bowl of mixed cereal there, and the milk's in the fridge. Get it down you quick and I'll meet you downstairs in ten minutes. That's twenty past six, OK.'

Sonny nodded and made for the kitchen. Patch headed for the stairs.

After eating the cereal, Sonny swilled the bowl and spoon, dried both, and put them back in their respective places. Then, using the clock on the wall in the kitchen, he allowed thirty seconds to get downstairs. At twenty past six exactly he was sitting at the bench in front of the chalkboard.

Patch handed him an army issue strapped watch, with a glow in the dark, sweeping second hand. 'I was going to give this to you this morning anyway, for you to time your run in the morning, or your run in the afternoon, or your run in the middle of the night for that matter. You can keep it. It'll remind you of the importance of timing. Precision timing.'

Sonny strapped the watch to his left wrist. 'Thank you,' he said, genuinely grateful for the gift.

Patch stood in front of the blackboard, arms folded. 'Right, the five mile. You're going to run it full on, no stops. You're as fit, probably fitter than a butcher's dog, so you should have it done between thirty to forty minutes. Remember, I want to see your recovery time improving, so don't cheat yourself. Full on. Go!'

Sonny leapt up from the bench and was out of the door of the barn in seconds. The morning light was now pretty good. He entered the wooded area, found the narrow path and was away, arms and legs pumping.

Compared to the uphill mountain run that he had been doing since the age of twelve, he found the cross-country terrain easy going. He fancied the thirty-minute finish rather than the forty minutes, so he pushed himself even harder. He loved the early morning country air. It reminded him of home. His mind was still a tortured wreck, but this kind of physical exercise was helping him to think about something else; even if it was for a short while.

He was on the home stretch when he checked his new watch. He guessed he could do the run in about thirty to thirty-two minutes, so he had another hard push on the legs for the last half mile. He burst through the woods into the courtyard area in the front of the barn and come to a stop. Checked his watch: thirty two minutes and a few seconds. Not bad.

He bent double with his hands on his knees and began the deep, even breath exercises to help his recovery. Then he was broadsided as if a bull had hit him. His assailant was all in black, with a black balaclava to match. They both went crashing to the gravel courtyard, with the black clad aggressor using Sonny as the cushion for the fall. He then gave the already short-breathed young man a couple of rabbit punches under his ribs, making him gasp for air. Sonny was flipped onto his stomach and his arms forced behind his back, and in no more than a second his wrists were cable tied together. A sharp punch to the kidneys finished him off and his ankles were soon bound the same way.

The aggressor then flipped Sonny onto his back and removed the balaclava. It was Patch! He sat on the gravel yard, legs crossed next to the trussed up young man. Both were breathing heavily.

'Jesus Christ, Patch! What the fuck? You nearly fucking killed me!' Sonny was panicking and as a result was spitting his words out, while coughing and gasping for breath. He let his head drop back onto the gravel. With his hands tied behind his back, his bodyweight was pulling on his arms, so he manoeuvred himself onto his side. Still doing his best to recover his breathing.

'If that was the man that you plan to go after, or one or more of his gang that just ambushed you, you would be dead already. Or very soon after. I gave you a book last night on hand to hand and unarmed combat, correct?' Patch had recovered from the quick fight and was now looking seriously at Sonny.

Sonny looked back at Patch like he'd suddenly grown another head. 'Yes, but fucking hell, Patch! I was tired, for crying out loud! I *will* read it, but no one can read a book like that before bed and be ready to deal with being fucking ambushed first thing in the morning, after a five mile run!'

'The title alone should have been enough for you to gain the suspicion as to what you would be introduced to today.' Patch reached into his trouser pocket and pulled out a very small, but razor sharp knife. He started shaking it at Sonny, while he was making his point.

'The people you are going to go after, they know you can fight, right? So, do you think that they are going to send you a letter or phone you up to let you know exactly when and where they are going to catch up with you?' He reached forward and cut the cable tie binding Sonny's ankles together.

'No, they damned well aren't. If you'd been careless and they'd found out where you were, they would use the element of surprise. You are a dangerous little bastard and they will not be taking any risks on sustaining any injuries if they can help it.'

Patch then cut Sonny's hands free, and he sat him on the gravel opposite. 'You need to think ahead. *You* need to know what *you* are going to do next. You must play out the whole scenario in your head. You must be certain that nothing can go wrong. This will influence what other people will do. Or what they are going to *have* to do if they have any hope of beating you.'

Patch picked himself up and offered a hand to Sonny, then hauled him to his feet. 'That book was a clue. If you had guessed that we would be doing unarmed combat techniques today, then maybe you would have got suspicious about me wanting you to go "full on" as you ran the five mile. Something might have seeded doubt in your mind.'

They walked to the front door of the barn. Sonny was still breathing heavily from the harsh and violent lesson he had just been taught.

'Over the next few weeks you will learn unarmed combat fighting techniques. This, coupled with what you already have, will make you one dangerous hombre. Mix this in with the ability to forward plan, to second guess. Create doubt in the mind of your enemies. You will then become their worst nightmare – trust me.' Patch unlocked the door and the pair went inside.

'Right, over to the large floor space. Unarmed, hand to hand combat. Let's have it.'

For the next few hours, Patch taught Sonny grappling techniques, instant stoppage punches to the throat and temple, submission holds and arm bars that could cause a person to pass out or choke, as well as solar plexus punches that when delivered, with varying force, could either knock the wind out of an adversary or kill them.

Sonny also learned how to use the fighting opponent's clothes as a weapon. For instance, if an opponent is wearing a pullover or a sweatshirt, grabbing a sleeve and pulling it, so the arm slips out, can leave a split second chance to deliver a knockout or killer blow. Tracksuit bottoms can be pulled down causing confusion, again gaining a second or two.

He was again reminded not to go charging in, but to absorb and observe what is happening or about to happen. A lot of fights can be ended before they even start. For instance, if an aggressor is pointing a finger to stress their superiority, the finger can be swiftly grabbed and snapped.

Some fights start with an aggressor standing with legs and arms apart, in typical arrogant or hooligan 'come on then' style. An extremely hard and forward snap kick to the knee, using bodyweight as extra force, can fracture the knee joint completely. Thus, ending the fight immediately.

If a fight turns into a wrestling match, an ear when gripped in a tight fist can be ripped right off, and when it is then shown to the opponent can cause utter fight ending horror.

Patch told Sonny that he had actually seen this done outside a bar in South Africa in a fight between a Special Forces soldier and a bar room bully. After a quick grappling match, the soldier jumped up and offered the ear, which he was holding between his thumb and forefinger back to the bully. The shock on the man's face was incredible, as he sat on the floor looking up at the soldier offering his own ear back to him! Patch didn't mention the fact that he was actually the soldier to Sonny. He didn't want to horrify him too much.

Patch continued to drill the mantra into Sonny over and over. 'When it comes to a straight fight, get it done quickly with extreme violence. End it as soon as possible.' Patch was more than a little impressed; in fact he was astounded, at how quickly Sonny could be shown a fighting move or technique, and then absorb it into his own unique fighting talent. With his world-class boxing skills he was going to become a beast to fight against.

Patch was quite happy to admit that in a very short time he wouldn't fancy coming up against the boy himself.

He smiled at the thought that Sonny would have made a superb SAS recruit. It was obvious that the boy was a superb athlete, and was a sponge for cunning and for learning. Not the kind of lessons that were taught in a school classroom, but the lessons that were taught by dangerous men, who did dangerous things.

The pair spent some time on the heavy bag, where Sonny displayed his amazing stamina with non-stop aggressive punching for five-minute sessions. It was around two in the afternoon when Patch called the daytime session to an end.

They went up the stairs to the living quarters and Sonny took himself to his room. He sat on the bed and then let himself fall backwards. Staring at the ceiling, he thought about the whole morning, but most of all he thought about Rhian. It was his eighteenth birthday next week, and he had always promised himself that on this day he would ask Rhian's father for permission to get engaged. They had no plans to get married too soon, but he wanted to show her parents that he really did love their daughter.

After he had showered and changed into a clean tracksuit and t-shirt, he joined Patch in the kitchen and helped prepare a huge bowl of pasta. After they had eaten, Patch made two mugs of tea and took them over to the settees, settling in one, with Sonny in the opposite one.

'I want to ask you something,' said Sonny. 'Well, talk to you about something, I think. I don't know.'

Patch took a sip of his tea and looked straight at Sonny. 'This is about your girl, Rhian, isn't it?'

Sonny nodded, slightly surprised that Patch had guessed.

'Don't worry, I have a plan,' said Patch, taking another sip of his tea.

CHAPTER FIFTEEN
Back in Touch

Rhian had been extremely worried since Sonny had spoken with her two weeks ago. She knew that he had got away safely and had not yet been taken by Byron Lewis. The very thought of that happening made her feel sick.

Rhian and Sonny had been together since they were children, and were utterly devoted to each other. Life without him was just impossible.

She knew that she was being watched constantly by Byron's crew, so that at least told her that her boyfriend had got away. But the not knowing was destroying her, and not hearing anything day after day was making it worse.

She got up at six. It was the same every morning. She would have a shower and a quick breakfast, and make her way down the fire escape and around to the front of the family newsagent's to open up and sort out the daily newspapers.

She loved her independence, and living on her own in the flat gave her this. Her father also thought it was a great idea, and had done nearly all the decorating himself. The family home was only a few doors down on the same street, and she would spend almost as much time there as she did in the flat. Rhian also loved working at the store. Every day, including Sunday, she would open up at six thirty, sort out the papers and run the counter until their only employee, Penny, an old family friend turned up at nine.

Being the only small general store in the village, the newsagent had always done very well. Her father paid her a generous weekly wage and, being an only child, it was a given that she would take over the business when her father eventually retired.

However, the last few days had been a misery.

Byron Lewis, Pete Sawyer, or both, would menacingly come into the shop and ask if she had heard from or seen Sonny. When she had told them that she hadn't, the advice was always the same. That it would be in her and her family's interest to say if, and when, she did hear from or see him.

A rambler entered the store. He appeared to be scouring the maps of the mountain walks and surrounding area. She could tell the ramblers from a mile off with their wax jackets, various styles of hat, army style cargo trousers, hiking boots and sticks. Alongside this he had a little rucksack for emergency rations and his ordnance survey maps stashed in the side pockets.

She managed to raise a smile as the rambler approached the counter with a couple of maps. But the smile disappeared as soon as the man spoke.

'Good morning, Rhian.' The rambler smiled at the young woman and then opened up one of the maps that he had brought to the counter. Rhian was taken aback that the stranger knew her name, seeing as she had never set eyes on him before in her life.

The rambler then started to point at various random places on the map as he spoke. 'I'm pretty certain that I haven't been seen since entering the village or this store, but let's play this safe shall we?'

He looked back at the map and then at the confused young woman. 'Sonny is safe and well. Now you point at the map.'

Rhian let out an audible sigh of relief. Her stomach lurched at the rambler's words and she had to bite her lip to stop herself from bursting into tears. She wanted to launch into a thousand questions, but managed to compose herself and pretend to observe the map and assist the friendly stranger.

He pushed an envelope towards her that had been hidden under another map lying on the counter. Rhian quickly grabbed it and threw it onto a shelf under the counter.

The rambler continued. 'May I say that you are indeed as naturally beautiful as he says you are, and that he will be thinking of you on his birthday tomorrow?'

Rhian smiled at the rambler's kind words. 'Has he been hurt?' she asked nervously.

The rambler smiled at the worried young woman. 'Absolutely not, in fact, he is getting better and stronger by the day. Most, but not all, will be explained in the letter. Read it, then burn it. It's very important that you burn it, OK.'

Rhian nodded, and the rambler folded up the map and paid. He then turned briskly away from the counter and left the store.

Patch had left the Land Rover about three miles outside the village. It was parked in a disused farm building that Sonny had mapped out for him. Patch had taken a quiet country walker's path and a circuitous route to get to the village. Patch and Sonny had spent the last week going over the finest details of Mynydd Du until Patch had a faultless map to follow, including a fast getaway route should he need it. Sonny had provided accurate times and routines of all Rhian's family, so that she would be completely alone when Patch made contact.

Patch reached the farm building without seeing another soul, and was soon on his way back to the midlands, thinking to himself that it had gone well.

Sonny heard the Land Rover coming up the lane and waited in the courtyard as Patch pulled up. He opened the driver's door and let Patch get out. He knew better than to immediately start pumping his mentor for information, and waited for Patch to speak when he was ready.

'Pretty girl, punching above your weight there, my friend, if you ask me,' he joked.

'Yeah well, I'm not asking you, am I?' Sonny retorted. 'How is she? How does she look? Is she safe?'

'Well, I'm not going to lie to you. She is safe, but she does look worried. My guess is that she's being watched constantly. After all, she is the only thing you have left to go back there for.' Patch thrust his hands into the pockets of his coat. He looked very serious.

'I'm being totally honest with you here. I am against you getting in touch with Rhian, until this is all over. I am concerned that Byron Lewis's patience will run out if he even suspects that you two are in touch. I'm sure she will get hurt if he finds out. Saying that, I also believe that your concentration will not be there if you don't, so I'm going along with it. But you both will do it my way or not at all. I don't want to live with the fact that I played a part in her getting hurt. Is that clear?'

Sonny nodded at the seriousness of Patch's words. He momentarily regretted his need to get in touch with Rhian, though he knew he was correct in thinking that she was desperate to see him again also, regardless of the danger it would put them both in.

Patch went into the barn and up the stairs with Sonny close behind. 'Now you wait until she has read the letter. I'm getting changed. You and I are going fighting on the five mile. Ten minutes.'

Rhian had waited until Penny turned up for work at 9.00am. Pete Sawyer had been in an hour earlier to buy some cigarettes and a newspaper. As always he had asked her the same question and, as always, had got the same answer.

She did truthfully have a trip to the wholesalers, so didn't feel as if she was making an excuse to Penny.

The letter the rambler had given her was stuffed down the back of her jeans. She didn't want to put it into her handbag or pocket in case one of those thugs decided to search her. It was horribly obvious that Byron had lecherous designs on her; the way he looked her up and down when he came into the store. He would love the chance to search her personally. The guy was thirty-something years old, overweight and always smelt of cigarette smoke and stale alcohol. Rhian shuddered at the thought.

She left the store and headed round to the back and up the fire escape to her flat. Nobody had seen the rambler talking to her in the store, but, just in case, she locked her door.

Going straight into the bathroom, and again locking the door, she sat on an old wicker chair that stood in the corner and carefully opened the envelope and unfolded the letter.

She smiled as she recognised her boyfriend's untidy writing immediately. *Never one of his strong points*, she thought. But she was relieved to receive anything from him right now so couldn't care less about the presentation of the words.

Sonny started the letter by telling her how much he missed her and wanted her to stay safe, but was desperate to let her know that he was OK. He told her about the rucksack that got stolen on the train. He left out most of the action details from the fight with the three men outside the pub, but explained that was how he came to meet Patch, the man who delivered the letter. He couldn't tell her where he was, but that he was safe, and Patch was helping him prepare 'For what I have to do if I want to live the rest of my life in peace.'

Those words alone scared Rhian to her very soul.

Mostly because she knew what they meant!

Sonny finished the letter by telling Rhian that he would phone her at the flat every week on Sunday morning around seven.

Sonny had told Patch that Byron and his crew 'collected' from the pubs and clubs on a Saturday night. He remembered his grandfather getting mad when the younger crew members became all macho and intimidating when they were collecting. Alf would constantly tell them that they had to be more businesslike.

Because of the obvious Saturday night indulgences when collecting, Patch's correct opinion was that the Lewis crew would not have such a keen eye for duty at 7.00am.

Rhian left the bathroom and went into the kitchen. She lit

a match from the box kept by the gas cooker and burnt the letter over the kitchen sink. She made sure it was completely destroyed before washing the ashes away down the plug hole.

She then left the flat and made her way to the old van for doing local deliveries. Her emotions were all over the place. She was relieved that Sonny was safe and that he had got in touch and would do so every week. Sonny was the love of her life and she knew that he felt the same. As far as she was concerned they would be together for life. Married with children – the whole works! Even the mere thought of that not happening filled her with dread. Her head was full of the 'what ifs' and 'maybes' on the drive to the wholesalers.

CHAPTER SIXTEEN
Six Weeks Later

Byron Lewis was beside himself with rage. He leaned back into the leather office chair in the scrapyard that he now owned, thanks to a fake bill of sale from Alf Wilton.

He looked out of the window at the piles of scrapped cars. Over the years he had learned that owning a scrapyard was an excellent front to mask *other* business ventures, but today he had a real problem gnawing away at him, and it was driving him up the wall.

Pete Sawyer sat in a chair in front of Byron. He was still tired from a Saturday night in Newport, consisting of copious amounts of cocaine, booze and a couple of young but willing fillies, arranged for him by his contact that catered for his special tastes.

He was now trying not to show how nervous he was at the news from DC Sharpe. Mainly because he knew, no matter what, Byron would continue to look for Sonny Wilton.

Eight weeks and there was not a single clue as to where the boy was. The boy had no family, no home, and no money. As far as Byron was concerned, this was no hope.

His crew had been leaning on and threatening anybody with a connection to the boy. They had even checked the hospitals. Everything had come to a dead end.

They had reached out to contacts in Cardiff and Swansea to see if he'd found sanctuary there, but again nothing. Sonny had disappeared, and this pissed Byron off immensely. Something was clawing away in the back of his mind. The organisation would never be safe until Sonny was dealt with.

DC Sharpe had just left and told him that his 'protected' time was well and truly up. He had fended off the suspicions from other officers that the Lewis crew were involved in the disappearance of Alf and his two business partners.

The story released, and encouraged by DC Sharpe, was Alf Wilton was so overcome with grief over the death of his beloved wife that he had chosen to retire from all his business activities, and had gone to live abroad with his grandson. Thanks to his huge network of legitimate, and not so legitimate contacts, he was able to do this and disappear into the sunset with no one knowing where he had gone. The same story was concocted for both Kelvin Harvey and Myron Vincent.

DC Sharpe had put in a half-hearted and non-urgent plea to various European missing persons organisations to make sure he looked like he was playing his part.

Byron had been unconsciously tapping his pen on the desk when, all of a sudden, he threw it at the window. 'Where the fuck are you hiding, you little shit?' He stood up sharply from the chair, sending it rolling back and crashing into the filing cabinet behind. 'I swear, Pete, I will fucking find him, and before I kill him I will make him suffer pain like he has never felt before.' Pete Sawyer nodded sagely at his boss and best friend. He had seen Byron's dark moods and violent tendencies many times before, but failing to find Sonny had driven him to a whole new level of evil intent.

Patch watched Sonny with more than a little pride and amazement. In the eight weeks since he had taken him in, this young man had excelled in everything that he was taught. If he was a Special Forces recruit his record would read 'exemplary'.

Some of his enthusiasm was down to the Sunday morning phone calls Sonny was making to Rhian. Knowing she was safe, and waiting for him, had somehow spurred him on, made him even more determined than he already was. She was the only one he had left, and he desperately wanted to be near her again, be able to protect her. Sonny had talked to Patch about their plans for the future, and Patch couldn't help but hope it all happened for them. They were obviously childhood sweethearts that were destined to spend their lives together.

Sonny's lock picking expertise were now as good as his own. He could look at a padlock, alarm lock, or door lock, decide his method, and have it opened in seconds. Once his first padlock was mastered, something just seemed to light up in his brain, and from there on in he was determined to become a master locksmith.

They had put his new-found skill into practice by entering a few premises across the city such as warehouses, where they perused the merchandise. In the same way they entered locked-up pubs at the dead of night, silently poured themselves a drink, and then left as ghosts like they had never entered.

The ultimate test was to make Sonny enter homes through the back door and exit through the front (or vice versa). These homes were particularly difficult as they knew the occupants were asleep upstairs. Sonny firstly had to observe the premises for as long as it took and then silently enter. He was to touch nothing and to move noiselessly through the downstairs. All closed doors had to be opened silently – a quick spray of odourless lock release to the hinges would normally stop any creaking. The first time Sonny started this test he was remarkably calm. He had been briefed by Patch that if he was compromised in the house 'flight' was the preferred option, and if 'fight' was unavoidable, only minimal combat was to be executed, so he could make a quick escape.

Patch needn't have worried. Sonny had developed surreptitious skills at entry and exit. He now had the ability to move as silently as a cat. He could control his breathing and would continually scan three hundred and sixty degrees. Patch had often thought to himself that Sonny could make a successful and lucrative cat burglar.

Sonny was practicing his take down, disable and tie-up techniques on a combat mannequin that Patch had bought some years back from an army surplus auction. The mannequin could stand in any position required and a knife or machete could be fitted into the hands for disarming combat practice. Techniques on take down, whether by surprise or in fight mode, could then be practiced. These would then be followed by disabling methods. For instance, trussing up an assailant by cable tie or gaffer tape.

Patch made Sonny practice with the mannequin to build stamina, and would make him repeat techniques over and over again – attack, take down, then disable. When Sonny was exhausted, Patch would take the place of the mannequin. The only difference was that Patch would fight back.

Often they would fight like territorial lions. It was almost as if they really were trying to seriously hurt each other.

More importantly, Sonny was starting to come out on top in these sessions, and no one was more pleased with this than Patch himself.

Patch had also been teaching Sonny unarmed combat in confined spaces: very small rooms, cars and lifts. A well-aimed elbow to the plexus, or the nose, from the driver's or passenger's seat can gain valuable time. Equally a pair of sunglasses, or a pen, can become a lethal weapon. Also, unclipping your aggressor's seatbelt, and then hoisting it around their neck causes panic and buys you time.

Patch was well aware that Sonny would very soon be combat ready, but he wasn't convinced that he was mentally ready. The boy was intent on killing another human being, but had never been remotely close to a combat situation where only one person would walk away.

The counselling sessions had been kept up almost every evening, but Sonny would never know peace again until he had avenged his grandparents. The shock of losing his grandmother was bad enough, but the memories of his grandfather's death. It was the mental torture that was driving him. He remembered the choking, gurgling death noises, while Sonny was hiding under the boxing ring, powerless to do anything, but listen.

Patch had a horrible feeling that something dark and nasty was about to happen; something that would light the fuse. He just hoped that no innocents would be in the way or get hurt when it happened.

CHAPTER SEVENTEEN
Lovers Tryst

Three weeks later, in early December, Patch was starting to sense impatience in Sonny. When Patch first thought of the idea, he immediately reproached himself. *Was he insane?* But the more he refined the plan in his mind, the more it made sense. He would unite the two sweethearts for a one-off secret tryst!

Logically, if Sonny could get close to Rhian and spend a few hours with her, it would give him peace of mind. He would then have more time to prepare himself mentally. Also, knowing that Rhian was safe would delay the inevitable carnage.

Patch did also consider a second option: the two of them could disappear to Australia or somewhere, but he knew that Sonny would forever be tortured. Justice had to been seen through!

For the next twenty-four hours he formulated a solid plan to get them together. The following evening, he told Sonny of his intentions, and Sonny, of course, agreed. He couldn't wait to get started!

*

On Sunday morning, Sonny phoned Rhian and, after checking that all was fine, he laid out the plan. The following Saturday, Rhian, and her best friend Lorna, would take a bus to Cardiff, followed by a train to Birmingham for Christmas shopping. Sonny told her to make the trip as public as possible. It was an absolute certainty that she would be followed. This seemed to scare her a bit, but Sonny told her to ignore her pursuer. If he (or she, but this was unlikely) followed her around the shops, she mustn't worry. She had nothing to hide!

Usually on Saturday Birmingham is packed and, with the festive period fast approaching, it would be even busier. Sonny told Rhian to head to the Bullring Shopping Centre and act perfectly normal – two young ladies enjoying retail therapy! He gave her a few shops to visit, and explained how the most dangerous part of the plan would happen.

*

Terry Owens was not at all happy to find out that he would be spending all day Saturday tailing Rhian Hughes around the shops in Birmingham. He had planned on having a few beers on Friday night, a good lie-in on Saturday, a full cooked breakfast around his mam's, a couple of hours in the bookies, and then back on the lash Saturday night.

Nevertheless, it was 9.00am on a Saturday and he was sitting on a train to Birmingham. Despite his early start, he still went for a few beers the night before, and his head was banging.

Rhian had already spotted him and offered him a dirty look. This changed everything; she knew that he was there, so the rest of the day was going to be a drag. He hated shopping at the best of times, but it was Christmas and the place was probably going to be packed. Besides, what would she do anyway? If the girl knew that she was being watched, she probably wouldn't do anything anyway.

Terry had never been good at tailing people and was surprised that Pete had asked him to do it. He was a doorman, a bloody good one too. Six-foot, good build; the kind of bloke with a face only a mother could love. This had usually helped as he worked the doors; some cheeky punters would have a look at his ugly mug and take a swerve, instead of taking him on.

But tailing people? Him? Really?!

'Orders from the boss, Tel. Just in case she's meeting that slippery little fucker,' Pete had told him.

But what is the point now? he thought. *If she's clocked me, she isn't going to lead me to him.*

The train pulled into Birmingham, New Street, and the two girls left the station and headed for the Bullring, arms linked and giggling like school kids. The Christmas lights were already switched on, and the crowds of shoppers had started to thicken.

Rhian appeared relatively calm, despite the fact that her stomach was doing somersaults and, in reality, she was absolutely terrified. Fifty yards behind her was Terry, his hands thrust deep into his leather jacket pockets, his face like thunder.

The two women entered the first few shops with enthusiastic gusto. Rhian's mind was obviously elsewhere, but she played along admirably – searching the shop rails for tops, trousers and dresses, and then trying them on.

Terry waited outside, a couple of shops down, his patience seriously stretched. He was also getting unimaginably bored at the thought of the rest of the day ahead of him, and it was only half past eleven.

It was approaching midday when Rhian and her friend entered a large clothes boutique. It had an entrance at the front, but more importantly an exit at the back, leading to the street behind.

As soon as they entered, it was obvious that their pursuer could no longer see them, which had been the case with most of the shops they had visited that morning. As they looked at the clothes on display, they slowly edged their way to the back of the shop.

Terry had fallen behind. He had been looking in the window of a shop specialising in body building supplements. He had taken his eyes off the ball for a second, but thankfully he spotted them enter a large clothes store.

As he stared intently at the store entrance an old man bounced off his large, solid frame. The man hit the shiny marble ground of the shopping terrace, scattering his bag's contents across the floor: fruit and vegetables, some fish fingers and a loo roll.

'Sorry, old fella, should look where you're going, shouldn't you?' Terry said. The old man looked shocked and was rubbing his back, looking rather distressed. Terry turned to leave, but immediately became aware of the scornful looks he was getting from people walking past. He quickly shot a glance at the shop. At least he knew where they were. He puffed out his cheeks and began to gather up the shopping for the old man.

Unbeknown to Terry, the old man was, in fact, retired Sergeant Robert (Bob) Checketts, aged seventy-four. His weathered features made him look even older, but his body was still as fit as a thirty-year-old, and bouncing off the burly doorman onto the floor had done him no harm at all.

Bob had been the senior instructor and trainer when Patch had joined the Special Forces, was his handler during covert operations, and they had remained firm friends ever since.

Bob had received a call from Patch asking him for his help and insisted on knowing the whole story. Bob could smell a tall story, and there was no way he would help if he thought he was being lied to. Bob, of course, did not like what Patch was undertaking, but after hearing Sonny's heartfelt plea, he offered his services.

Almost at the same time as Terry had confronted Bob, the two young women left the shop by the back exit.

Patch was waiting for them outside. He quickly approached them and smiled reassuringly at Rhian. She recognised him immediately. 'Hello again, thanks for the note,' she said.

'Oh, hello. No bother.' He smiled. 'Now follow me.' Patch briskly headed off down the street – but they had only walked a hundred yards when Patch turned, and quickly ushered them into the entrance of a small private hotel. Once inside, he thrust a key into Rhian's hand. 'Room number four,' he said. 'Sonny is waiting for you. Four knocks on the door, and let yourself in. You have two hours together, maximum.'

He then turned to Rhian's friend and pointed to an armchair next to a payphone. 'Can you please stay there until the phone rings? When it does, it means the time is up. Go and get your friend. Remember, four knocks.' Rhian's friend nodded, looking slight out of her depth.

He turned back to Rhain. 'I know it will be tough, but you must leave that room immediately.'

Rhian nodded eagerly, and she was gone, heading straight to room four. Patch turned his attention back to Rhian's friend, and pointed outside. 'I will be outside five minutes after the call. Look for a green Land Rover. Got it?'

She nodded, then reached inside her handbag for a few magazines and waved them in front of him. 'Got it, no problem. Thank you for helping my friends. I'm Lorna by the way,' offering her hand.

Patch smiled, but didn't take her hand.

'Oh, OK. It's like that, is it? Always the bridesmaid, never the bride,' she said, edging her way back to the armchair.

Patch looked seriously at the young woman. 'We've got to pull off the rest of this stunt first, and then I'll breathe a little easier.' He turned and left quickly, heading straight back to the shopping precinct.

As he entered, he noticed that Bob was still occupying the pursuer, who had a bouncer look about him. *Clever boy*, Patch thought. The bouncer was getting more and more irate. A crowd had surrounded him, as well as a security guard. The bouncer was holding his hands in the air. 'I did not hit him,' he said, but the crowd was not convinced.

As soon as Bob spotted Patch, the old soldier touched the peak of his flat cap and, in return, Patch rubbed his chin in reply. Everything seemed to be going to plan.

So far.

Patch would now follow the follower. He was a

surveillance expert, and keeping up with this buffoon was not going to be a problem.

Patch was gambling that the bouncer wouldn't call his boss straight away about being given the slip. He would look for them first. That's why timing was so important for Sonny and Rhian's short reunion.

Rhian quickly made her way down the hallway. Room 1 to the left, room 2 to the right, room 3 to the left, and then she was standing outside room 4. She knocked on the door four times, her hands shaking so badly she almost dropped the key. She was deliriously excited to see Sonny again, but aware enough to remove the key from the lock, before she entered the room. She pushed the door open and there, standing by the window wearing a blue short-sleeved linen shirt and a pair of faded jeans, was the man that she wanted to spend the rest of her life with. The immediate outpouring of love and relief was too much, and she threw the door shut, dropped the jacket she had been carrying, and rushed into his arms. Burying her head in his chest she sobbed with relief.

Sonny wrapped his powerful arms around Rhian and held her close to him. He stroked her long hair, drinking in the smell of her perfume that he had missed so much. He had been pacing the room like a caged animal all morning, and when he had finally heard the four knocks on the door it took a great deal of control to stop himself rushing across the room, and ripping it from its hinges. Rhian looked into Sonny's eyes. As they kissed,

Rhian stroked his handsome face and began to unbutton his shirt. Sonny put his hand on hers.

'We can wait,' he whispered. 'Until this is all over.' Rhian brushed his hand aside and carried on until the shirt was fully open. She slipped it from his shoulders. Sonny had always had a great physique as far as Rhian was concerned, but as she run her hands down his chest and stomach, she could tell that he had become stronger, more muscular and athletic.

Sonny reached behind Rhian's neck and unzipped her dress. She let it drop to the floor. He then swept her up into his arms, carried her to the large bed and gently laid her down on it. Together they slipped under the duvet.

They had never previously gone this far but, without saying it out loud, it felt right. For the next hour they made love; with both passion and sometimes clumsy virginal naivety, but with a love for each other that knew no bounds.

After they both had showered, with Rhian being careful to not let her hair get wet, they got dressed and Sonny told her his plans. 'This will all be over, hopefully sooner rather than later,' he said.

Rhian desperately wanted to tell Sonny not to go through with his plans, but she knew that it would be useless. If he didn't do what he thought he had to do, Sonny would be miserable for the rest of his life.

But she also feared for his life.

'Byron Lewis is a murderous lunatic,' she said. 'How do you expect to walk back into Mynydd Du, and do all this by yourself?'

'I need to try and Patch says he will help me.'

They cuddled up and talked about the life they were going to build together once this was over. Two young lovers, enjoying the little time that they had left in room 4.

Terry was fuming. Once the silly old sod had got his shopping back, and withdrawn his claim of violence, Terry headed straight over to the clothes store the two girls had gone into. He stood in the doorway looking around. There were a few customers there, but no a sign of Rhian and her friend.

He walked through the store, stopped, listened at the changing rooms, but there was nothing. He used the rear exit and looked up and down the street. There were no shops, so he re-entered the store and left by the front. By now the precinct was alive with Saturday Christmas shoppers. *Where are they?* he thought. He scanned all the shops, trying to think like a woman, but finally all he could do was guess.

The thought of phoning Byron or Pete and telling them that he had lost them made him feel physically sick. No, he would find them, of that he was certain.

After ninety minutes of visiting nearly every shop in the Bullring, Terry was extremely angry and worried about what to do next. He sat down on a bench outside the shopping complex, pulled out his cigarettes and matches, and lit one up.

A few minutes of respite.

Taking a look at his watch, almost 3.00pm, he decided to head back to the train station. He'd concluded that Rhian's friend was always out on a Saturday night – he'd seen her queuing. So, it was plausible that she would be looking to catch the train to Cardiff no later than 4.00pm. It would take him about twenty minutes to get to the station.

Patch had watched the bouncer rush around the Bullring for nearly two hours. If it hadn't been such a serious and time precious situation he would have found it somewhat hilarious. Considering that the big idiot was supposed to be clandestinely following the two young women, he was now charging around the place like the proverbial bull! He may as well have been shouting their names out with a bullhorn!

Right now, Patch was stood beside a phone box about a hundred yards away from the bouncer, who looked genuinely panicked. Patch had seen this kind of behaviour many times before. Watching his body language, it was obvious that the bouncer was out of ideas and was now heading for the railway station.

Patch quickly made a call from a phone box, as he tried to second-guess the route the bouncer would take.

The first ring almost scared Lorna half to death. She dropped her magazine and snatched the phone from its cradle. 'Hullo, it's Lorna,' she stammered.

'Five minutes, go.' Patch quickly barked on the other end. He then hung up.

Lorna checked her watch. It was coming up to 3.00pm. She hurried to room 4 and knocked the door four solid times.

Sonny and Rhian leapt up from the bed and immediately fell into each other's arms. They held each other tightly.

'I love you, Sonny Wilton, I always will. If you have to go through with this, then do it. Just make sure you come back to me. You know I'll be waiting.' She then slipped a hair band onto his wrist, to leave something of 'her' with him. They kissed one final time and then she let go. She picked up her jacket from where she had dropped it, and took one last look at the man that she loved. 'Please make sure, that next Christmas will be ours.' She opened the door and left. All of this took no more than thirty seconds.

Sonny sat back down on the bed and buried his head in his hands. He didn't shed any tears. He just felt helpless. He could do nothing but stay in this room until Patch came to fetch him. Someone else would take care of Rhian and Lorna, but who better than Patch Rawlings, ex-Special Forces. Sonny allowed himself a rare smile. He made the hair band that Rhian had given him snap on his wrist, and then threw himself back onto the bed.

Rhian and Lorna hurried into the hotel foyer and gathered up their shopping bags. Lorna checked her watch. Just two minutes had passed since Patch's phone call, so they stood for a moment opposite each other; both looking a bit bewildered and shocked by it all.

Lorna broke the silence. 'Is he OK? How does he look?' she asked her best friend.

'He's fine, staying with a friend. I'll tell you more later,' Rhian lied in reply. She could not tell the whole story to her friend. Not yet anyway. Nobody could know anything; then nobody would get hurt.

They heard a vehicle pull up outside, and a quick glance out of the window confirmed that it was the Land Rover. The two women quickly rushed out of the hotel and straight into the back. Patch appeared, breathing heavily.

'Been out running?' asked Lorna.

'Something like that,' replied Patch.

After less than five minutes driving over the speed limit, Patch pulled over and signalled to the young women that they were on the move. They jumped out of the Land Rover and Patch led them down a narrow alleyway, and out onto a busy street not far from the train station.

'Right, quickly, in here.' He guided the pair to the doorway of a neat little Chinese restaurant, ushering them inside and followed behind. The two women were immediately led to a table in front of the large window by a waiter, and before they had time to even glance at a menu, two plates of steaming noodles were put in front of them, as well as two bottles of cola and a large bowl of prawn crackers. They were encouraged to eat. Lorna was happy to oblige; she was starving. Rhian was far from hungry, but was more than willing to play along.

Patch leaned over the table and pointed across the road to the busy high street. 'In the next couple of minutes your shadow will be storming down that road with a face like thunder. You two just act normal and we'll see what happens. After you've finished your lunch you can make your way to the train station. By the way, the Chinese food here is the best in Birmingham.'

He then left the women to their noodles. He walked into the kitchen and hugged Chin, another old army friend, and owner of the restaurant.

'Thanks,' he said. 'I owe you one.'

Terry had only ever been to Birmingham twice before, so had to follow the signs back to the train station. As he walked down the busy high street, he found he constantly had to dodge past Christmas shoppers struggling with shopping bags. He was not a happy fellow. *Would they even be at the station?* he thought. *They could have taken an earlier train home.* Byron would have his guts for garters if he found out.

Terry decided to look at the timetables and keep an eye on the platforms. If he was lucky the girls would come to him.

If not, he would be in for the biggest beating of his life. Byron would certainly have a spotter at the bus station in the village, and if Rhian and her friend got off a bus without him close behind, there would be hell to pay. Byron was obsessed with Sonny bloody Wilton, and if he'd thought that the girl had given him the slip… Terry pushed the thought out of his mind. This *had* to work.

He reached the pelican crossing and stopped, waiting for the green light. He glanced across to the other side of the road. There they were – sitting in the window, scoffing down a Chinese! 'Thank fuck for that!' he said very loudly.

The violent thug in him wanted to find a rock and put it through the window. Instead, he gathered his composure, and when the beeping sounded for him to cross the road, he attempted his best nonchalant stroll to the other side. When the two women saw him, he was going to give them the impression that he knew exactly where they were, and where they had been.

He did, inevitably catch their attention as he walked past the restaurant. He gave them a quick nod. They in return offered him a look of indifference.

All Terry had to do now was make sure he arrived back home at the same time as the two girls. He would report to Byron that no strange happenings had occurred in Birmingham and, as a result, avoid any broken bones or lost teeth. Then he was then going to get drunk. He had earned it as far as he was concerned.

Patch, carrying a large brown paper bag of gorgeous smelling Chinese food, walked right past the bouncer on his way back to the Land Rover. He was whistling quietly to himself when he reached his vehicle. He put the Chinese food in the sealed storage box in the back to keep it warm. He then leaned against the bonnet to contemplate the last few hours. *How did it go? Did anything not go to plan? Would he have done anything differently?*

He opened the driver's door and thought, *Nope, like clockwork, even if I do say so myself.*

CHAPTER EIGHTEEN
Buying Time

Christmas came and went without drama or celebration at the barn. Patch thought it best to let the occasion go without fuss, as Sonny would have only thought how Christmas should have been. Patch had spent much of life in countries that never celebrated Christmas anyway, so he wasn't particularly bothered.

It had been over five months since Sonny had disappeared from Wales and eight weeks since the lovers tryst. Sonny seemed happy to hone his new-found skills, knowing that Rhian was safe and would be waiting for him.

Since this meeting, the work rate had intensified greatly, and the results were nothing short of frightening. To the ordinary citizen, Sonny's hand to hand combat and ambushing techniques were truly horrific to watch or witness. Sonny and Patch would fight each other, with the serious intent to inflict severe harm – and deep bruises and spilt blood became the norm.

Patch, rightly or wrongly, convinced Sonny to think of Byron Lewis when fighting, and the results were spectacular to say the least.

At first, Sonny would fight with a furious rage, but more

often than not, he would make mistakes. Patch would use these opportunities to gain the upper hand, and bring the young man down.

Afterwards, during counselling sessions, Patch taught the skill of controlled aggression and maintaining eye contact with an opponent.

'Calm eye contact sends a signal of confidence that an opponent will find unnerving,' he said. Then, with extreme force, aggression and effectiveness, you can end the fight as quickly as possible.'

Patch created all kinds of scenarios, such as being discovered in a house after forced entry. He was shown how to use furniture as obstacles, and how household items could be used as weapons.

At the dead of night, Sonny was ambushed when he undertook his five mile run in the woods. He learned how to control his breathing, so not to give away his position.

Patch sometimes starved Sonny of food for forty-eight hours, and then staged an ambush or a fight. This taught Sonny how to end a fight quickly, even if you are hungry or thirsty.

Patch soon became confident in Sonny's ability to carry out his intentions of revenge. He had replaced his inner torment with a controlled determination. The boy was more than combat ready. Patch was carrying the bruises as testament to that.

But did Sonny have the mental capability to carry the plan through? Patch had seen fully-trained SAS soldiers unable to make the kill. These soldiers were then deemed a liability to the safety of their comrades, with their Special Forces careers coming to a swift end.

To be honest, Patch had never trained anyone with a mission like Sonny's, but he had come through with flying colours. If it had been a military situation, Patch would be more than confident that this soldier was ready to serve.

But Sonny's War was a whole new ball game. Would he survive his mission? Would he go on a murderous rampage with no regard for his own life? Or would he take out the players one by one, by stealth and cunning. In his mind, he knew. There would be a happening – a catalyst that would trigger everything. There wasn't an 'if' but a 'when', and all would unravel after that. Hell was going to cut loose! Of that he was certain.

*

It was Saturday night and Byron was working at *The Night Owl* club; one of many that he ran the door service at, consisting of protection and drugs. He also owned most of the spirits on the optics behind the bar. Business was good.

He normally enjoyed himself there. It was popular with the ladies, especially when he had girls vying for his attention. If nothing came up, he would settle for a working girl. He owned them, so it was his right. He wasn't fussed.

But tonight, he was in the foulest of moods. Coked up to the eyeballs, but not enjoying the evening. Byron's cocaine intake was legendary. People couldn't understand how he hadn't dropped dead, given the amount of 'Charlie' he'd put up his nose. In reality, Byron was a cocaine-fuelled unhinged maniac.

Tonight the coke was having the reverse effect on his mood; he was just getting paranoid and irritable by the minute. It was strange, as things were actually good! Money was pouring into the organisation. Supplying the local pubs and clubs with drugs was making him vast amounts of cash. The pills and powder from Amsterdam had gone down well. And car ringing and car container thefts were on the up.

So, why wasn't he grinning from ear to ear?

Instead he looked across the dance floor, where Rhian and her friends were doing their best moves to *West Ends Girls* by the Pet Shop Boys.

Sonny Wilton had evaded him for over five months, and it was now driving him insane. He was sure that Rhian had been up to something on her so-called Christmas shopping trip to Birmingham. Byron had hauled Terry in three times afterwards, and had grilled him until his head was spinning, but Terry was adamant that he hadn't let them out of his sight for a minute.

Terry was threatened with violent repercussions to himself and his family if Byron ever found that the women had given him the slip, but Terry stuck to his story.

But Byron, even without any proof, was still convinced that something went down with Rhian and Sonny, and it was gnawing away at him.

*

Rhian decided not to dance to *Ebeneezer Goode* by The Shamen, and convinced her friends to leave the dance floor. As they pushed through the crowd to get back to their seat, Rhian was getting a slight headache. She didn't normally get drunk because of her early morning starts, and had stuck to drinking half pints of orange juice and lemonade. Her headache wasn't alcohol-induced then!

For a while the chat and gossip had been loud and raucous around the table, until… Rhian turned around to what had been an empty chair and found herself face-to-face with Byron Lewis. His eyes were bloodshot; full of rage, although the rest of his face was calm. His lips were tightly pursed, as if he was thinking what to say next; choosing the best words to terrify the young woman.

Rhian wore a plain white mini-dress, even though it was late January. It always got very hot in the club as the night wore on.

Byron looked her up and down and ran his tongue around his lips. 'Having a good night?' he asked, completely ignoring everyone else around the table. In return, the rest of the group purposely busied themselves in fake conversations, so not to engage or antagonise the gangster that had intruded upon them.

'Yes, we are, thank you,' Rhian replied as confidently as she could.

'It's freezing out there. Do you want me to give you a lift home later? My car's just around the corner.'

Byron moved closer to the young woman, until his face was only about twelve inches from hers. It felt like he was almost staring into her soul, like a devil that could viciously lash out at her without a second thought. 'No thanks,' she replied, her token confidence being replaced by an uneasy fear. 'Four of us will share a taxi, same as we always do.' She did, in fact, intend to get a taxi by herself a little earlier. She had to be up early in the morning for the Sunday papers, but she wasn't going to tell him that.

Byron leaned even closer to Rhian, and through gritted teeth and with stale cigarette breath, said: 'Where is he? I know you know where he is. If I find out that you've been lying to me I will fucking kill you, and everyone else you know. Do you understand?' '*Perfectly*!' Rhian replied loudly, throwing her chin up in a weak display of defiance.

'So, where is he?' Byron persisted again.

'I don't know,' Rhian retorted, trying desperately not to panic.

'But you would definitely tell me if you did, wouldn't you, Rhian?' His eyes appeared to be searching hers for clues.

'I *don't* know,' she said again.

Byron spoke quietly, so no one else could hear. 'You do know. And I know you know. So, don't fuck me around!'

Rhian shrugged her shoulders. Inside she was almost crying, but her defiance remained intact. Byron leaned back in the chair again, still eyeballing the now visibly trembling girl. He stayed there for what felt like an eternity. A fake smile plastered on his face.

'You all enjoy the rest of your night,' he said, with a sarcastic and condescending tone as he looked around at everyone sat at the table. He tossed a ten pound note on the table. 'Get a drink on me,' he said.

'Oh, thanks,' said the girls in unison. All except Rhian. *I'm not taking your blood money*, she thought.

'Be seeing you again, Rhian. You take care now.' He adjusted and buttoned up his blazer, then turned and walked through the crowd, which parted like the Red Sea.

When she was sure he had gone, Rhian let out a huge sigh of relief. Lorna came around the table, sitting in the chair now vacated by Byron. She put an arm round her. Rhian's night had been well and truly spoiled. 'I'm getting a taxi,' she announced.

'It's a bit early,' said Lorna. 'I just want to get home.'

'Do you want me to come with you,' said Lorna, reaching for her bag.

'No, I'll be fine. It's only midnight. You stay. You've got nearly two hours left of drinking and dancing, I'll be fine.'

'Honest?' asked Rhian.

'Yes, don't worry. Enjoy yourself.'

Rhian made her way to the exit. The doorman gave her a cold stare as he held the door open for her to leave. *Ghostbusters* by Ray Parker Jnr had started to boom out, and she looked back to see her friends heading back to the dance floor. She smiled and waved to them, then left the club in favour for the cold, dark street. It had been raining. She buttoned up her coat and pulled the hood over her hair

The taxi rank was fifty yards down the road, so she quickened up her pace to avoid getting wet. She didn't have a chance to cry out as a large figure came out of the shadows and wrapped a powerful arm around her neck. Another hand clamped over her mouth and nose, and she was dragged backwards into the dark alley.

CHAPTER NINETEEN
Getting Worried

Sonny was out of bed at 5.45am, the same time as every other morning – five minutes early! He dragged himself into his tracksuit bottoms, and prepared himself for the five mile run through the woods.

He went into the kitchen and poured himself a small glass of milk, drinking it quickly. Quickly he jogged down the stairs and into the gym to do his stretches.

He always enjoyed the freedom running had brought him, and the cross-country terrain of the five mile was liberating. The canopy of the trees, the sound of the leaves crunching beneath his feet, and the up and down hilly terrain of the woods, all made him feel like he was running in the wild.

Today, however, was his phone call day to Rhian, and it didn't matter what instructions Patch gave him, he would fly round the five mile, be showered and on the phone by 7.00am.

Sonny wasn't overly concerned when she didn't answer the first call. This had happened a couple of times before. Sometimes the Sunday paper delivery ran late. Sometime a customer would keep her talking.

Sonny did, however, become a little concerned when there was no reply twenty minutes later. He could feel the panic building up in his stomach when there was still no reply at quarter to eight.

Patch was in the kitchen preparing breakfast. He usually instigated a counselling session after Sonny had been on the phone to Rhian, to talk through any concerns he might have, or just to listen to any bits of their conversation Sonny may have wanted to share with him. This helped Patch to judge where Sonny's head was at, but when Patch failed to hear any conversation at all going on, the clanging bells of doom started to ring in his head.

Sonny turned to look at Patch. He had panic in his eyes, a look of not knowing what to do next. Patch went over and took the phone off him, placing it on the table in front of them both.

'Every fifteen minutes. You *will* get an answer eventually.' He dragged a chair over to the corner and they sat opposite each other.

Every fifteen minutes Sonny tried Rhian's number. Every time there was no reply. He kept pulling on the hair band on his wrist, the sting as it rebounded back adding to his angst and anger.

The phone was answered at ten fifteen by Rhian's father, Arthur. He sounded both solemn and heartbroken.

'Mr Hughes, it's Sonny,' he quickly blurted down the line.

'I know, son,' he answered, his voice shaking with emotion.

Sonny could hear Rhian's mother sobbing in the background and dreaded what he was about to hear. 'Please, tell me what's happened. I've been trying to call Rhian since seven.'

'Yes, I know. We've been at the hospital since six this morning.'

For some strange reason, Sonny's mind momentarily went to 6.00am, when he was enjoying his run through the woods and looking forward to talking to Rhian.

'Someone found our Rhian in an alley at five this morning.'

Sonny tried not to cry, winded by the news. 'Is she dead?' he asked.

'They thought she was dead. Not just from her injuries but the cold. She had been lying there for hours.'

Sonny felt slightly relieved that Rhian was alive. 'Injuries? What injuries?' Sonny couldn't disguise the trembling anger in his voice. Patch buried his head in his hands.

'She's been beaten badly, Son. She has a broken jaw, cheek bone and eye socket. The surgeon says that the monster that did it stamped on her face.'

The line went silent.

'Mr Hughes, are you there?' asked Sonny, who could hear sobbing at the other end of the line.

'Sorry, Son. Had to turn the radio down.'

The line went silent again. Sonny went over to the stairs, trailing the phone wire behind him, and sat down. 'She has a broken left arm in two places, broken ribs and a broken right leg below the knee, and she's cut and bruised from head to toe,' said Mr Hughes.

Sonny struggled to get air into his lungs. His mouth had completely dried and it felt like his throat was constricting.

Mr Hughes continued with his devastating news. 'She

had an operation this morning and they say she's stable, but under heavy sedation.

'Where is she?' Sonny asked through gritted teeth. 'University Hospital, Cardiff,' the heartbroken father replied.

There followed a silence that seemed to go on for ages. Both men could hear the other breathing down the phone line.

Mr Hughes broke the silence. 'You know who is responsible for this, Son, and I believe he did this himself, not one of his bloody henchmen?'

'Yes, I think so,' Sonny replied with equal emotion. 'Byron.'

'I may be an old man, but I am going to make him pay for this. One way or another.'

Sonny stood up and spoke calmly to make sure that his words would get through to Mr Hughes.

'Mr Hughes, you know what happened to my grandparents, and what most likely happened to his best friends. Well, I've been preparing myself these last few months to get retribution for them. I urge you to do nothing. I will sort this out!'

'You promise to make that evil bastard pay for what he's done,' Mr Hughes said with a hiss.

'I promise,' Sonny replied. Then hung up the phone.

CHAPTER TWENTY
Going Back

For the next few hours, Patch had to think on his feet. Moment by moment, minute by minute, hour by hour. Here was the catalyst that he had dreaded coming – the trigger that would set off a murderous chain of events.

Even Patch, with his many years of combat experience, never thought that Byron would be reduced to beating a young girl almost to death, to force his enemy out into the open.

Sonny's mood switched from being distraught to feeling responsible, to a volcanic rage. He stood outside the barn shouting at the sky.

'I'm going to make that bastard pay. He's fucking dead!' shouted Sonny, not caring who could hear him. Patch took him by the arm, and led him back into the house.

For the next few hours, Patch tried to calm Sonny down. 'You need to think this through, Sonny. It's exactly what Bryon wants. If you go there in this state of mind you'll be signing your death certificate. We need to take stock. You must use everything I have taught you. Control your emotions,' said Patch, who felt sure that Byron was already preparing for a showdown.

Patch, of course, was confident in Sonny's ability to beat any man in a straight fight, but Byron wasn't any man. He was a monster!

To beat this monster, Sonny would need to employ cold, calculated tactics. Byron Lewis must die! But how? Sonny could end up in prison for a very long time, and this could be worse than not doing anything. He would still be separated from Rhian!

*

It was 4.00pm by the time Patch finally talked Sonny into relative calm. They sat opposite each other, thinking. They didn't have a cast iron plan, but they knew that time was of the essence. Sonny would head back to Mynydd Du, with Patch having to think on his feet, hour by hour.

Sonny wanted to leave that evening, but Patch attempted to delay him for a couple of days, even though he had to admit that he would have reacted immediately if it had been him in the same position. Strike while the iron was hot, but this was different. He had so much to lose.

Together they packed a large rucksack, and Patch gave Sonny an envelope containing two thousand pounds in cash, which he accepted gratefully. He promised to pay it back later.

'I know you will,' said Patch.

Sonny was in no mood for food, but still had a light meal with Patch. It made sense to eat something. He didn't really know when he would eat again!'

It was dark when they set off for the train station. On the way

Patch and Sonny talked about all the different ways in and out of town.

'You can't get spotted,' reaffirmed Patch. This was rule number one.

'I want to go and see Rhian,' pleaded Sonny.

'You can't do that, Sonny. Not under any circumstances!'

'I'd be careful,' said Sonny.

'No, Sonny, it's suicide. They probably won't be expecting you to react this quickly. They don't know where you are. They may think that you are already dead. Or abroad. If so, getting back to the town would take you some time. You currently have the element of surprise on your side, but this is a card you only hold once. Once you show it, it's gone, so don't waste it.'

Patch had noticed a calmness that had come over the young man. He had seen this before in his army career. Soldiers just about to go into combat, reaching into their inner thoughts: planning and plotting, playing the moves out in their mind. He could tell that Sonny was readying himself for the next few days.

The journey to the train station took about half an hour.

It was agreed that Sonny would catch the eight thirty to Cardiff and then a bus to Mynydd Du, getting off as far away as was reasonably possible. Then he would find a good hideout in the countryside, where he could slowly trek into the town. From then on he would be on his own.

Patch parked the Land Rover in a side street near the train station. Both men got out and Sonny, dressed in his outdoor walking gear, offered his hand to Patch. 'Thank you for everything. I'll be in touch when it's over.'

Patch grabbed his hand and pulled him into a hug. 'I'm not going to ask you if you really want to do this, but please promise me to use the tools I have given you. Make your decisions from a professional and calculated perspective. With your head, not with your heart. Now go and get it done.'

Sonny threw on his rucksack. He gave a nod to his mentor for the last six months, then turned and headed to the entrance, disappearing quickly into the crowd.

Patch got back into the Land Rover, fired it up and headed for home. He would be keeping his ears and eyes on any television or radio news that may or may not be coming out of Wales in the next few days.

For sure.

CHAPTER TWENTY-ONE
Back Home

The train to Cardiff was already waiting at the platform. Sonny purchased a one-way ticket and boarded the end carriage. From a distance the train appeared quite full, with mostly shoppers and day trippers. After helping a lady with a pram, Sonny took a corner seat. He could see as far as the next carriage, and was confident that there would be no dramas on this part of the journey but, just in case, he needed to be alert. With no apparent threat he calmed himself down.

Twang! This time he would not go to sleep though. Twang! He didn't want to lose his bag again. Twang! Instead he thought about Rhian. Twang! She was lying in hospital because of him. Twang! That bastard, Byron, deserved to die! Twang! Sonny realised he had been pulling viciously on Rhian's hair band. Twang! His wrist was red raw with pain. He stopped himself, pulling the cuff of his jacket down over his hand.

There were three stops before Cardiff: Bristol Parkway, Bristol Temple Meads and Newport. All were uneventful, with people mostly getting off, but Sonny stayed alert anyway, scanning the platforms and studying the faces of anybody entering the carriage. He could feel his heart pounding when he realised that the next stop was his. Cardiff.

It was 10.30pm when the train pulled in, and nearly all the passengers gathered their belongings together in preparation to disembark. Sonny joined in, fitting his rucksack onto his back. He swapped his baseball cap for a woollen beanie, and pulled it tight over his head and zipped his coat up to his chin.

As soon as the carriage door was open he stepped onto the platform, making sure he was amongst the crowd of passengers heading for the exit. He surreptitiously took a look down the platform, and right at the end he spotted one of Lewis' goons, leaning against a wall. He had probably been there for most of the day, and his enthusiasm had long gone. He didn't even raise his head from his newspaper to study the passengers leaving the station, being more interested in yesterday's football results than looking out for his boss's nemesis. Sonny kept an eye on him, as he slipped through the exit and out of the station.

Casually, but as quickly as he could, he found a red telephone box away from the station. After feeding it some coins, he dialled Rhian's number. Arthur Hughes answered after the first ring.

'Mr Hughes, it's me. I'm in Cardiff and I need to see Rhian.'

'Already ahead of you, Son – although I didn't think you'd come so soon.'

'It's time, Mr Hughes.'

'Call Holly Thomas. She's one of Rhian's old school friends and was with her on Saturday night. Holly's a ward nurse at the hospital. She knows you'll be coming and says she can slip you in for a couple of minutes. Here's her number.'

Sonny had a pen and small pad ready in his jacket pocket,

and quickly wrote down the number, reading it back to be sure he had got it right.

'Sonny, be careful.'

'I will, Mr Hughes – and thank you.' 'Please be careful, Sonny. We care abo— 'I know, Mr Hughes,' interrupted Sonny.

'And it's Arthur or Arty from now on, OK?' 'OK, Mr, sorry… Arthur, I'll be in touch.' 'I'll be here, or at the shop.'

They both hung up.

Although it was nearly 11.00pm Sonny decided to phone Holly straight away. He was a little surprised, but relieved that she answered after a couple of rings.

'Someone rather nasty has been watching the front entrance, Sonny. A few of my colleagues have spoken to him and asked him to move, but he was still there when I finished my shift this afternoon. I guess he's waiting for you. It's best you meet me around the back at 6.30 tomorrow morning.'

'OK, thanks, Holly. How is she?'

'Not good. She's under heavy sedation, so she probably won't know you're there. Be prepared for the worst, Sonny.'

Sonny could feel his heart thumping as he listened to Holly's words of warning. *It's all my fault*, he thought. *I'm going kill that fucker.* Pause. He stopped to remember Patch's training. He filled his lungs with cold night air and slowly blew it out, calming his mind. He spoke quietly. 'I just want to see her. Even if she doesn't know I'm there. I need to see her.'

'I know, Sonny. She's been worried about you too.

I'll see you in the morning, bye.'

She hung up. Sonny replaced the receiver and punched a glass panel repeatedly, until blood was running down his knuckles.

Sonny stepped out of the phone box and checked his watch. 11.04pm. Traffic was thinning out and the night was getting cold. It would take around forty-five minutes to get to the Heath Hospital, but there were no buses. Sonny knew there was a Salvation Army hostel nearby. Both he and Patch had been diligent in their research! Sonny was still very wired, but thought it was best to make his way there.

He was welcomed by a lovely old lady in her seventies who was dressed in the traditional Salvation Army uniform. She was sitting at a small reception desk and introduced herself as Sylvie. He, in return, told her that his name was Joseph. Sonny did actually look the part in his big raincoat, outdoor boots and his beanie pulled tight over his head. He spun the old lady a yarn that he was passing through on his way to Pembroke, and she gave him a sympathetic look that said she had heard it all before.

Sylvie led him to a large room with six single beds. Three were already occupied with men who appeared to be fast asleep. The unmistakable smell of sweaty socks and damp clothes hung in the air. Sonny chose an empty bed nearest to the door for quick evacuation if needed. Sylvie pointed silently to a door at the other end of the room with a sign saying, 'Toilet and washroom', and then left him to it.

Sonny sat on the bed and pulled the beanie off his head, stuffing it into his coat pocket. He took his boots off as quietly as he could, and then tied them up by the laces to the top of the wrought iron headboard above the pillows. Now, if one of the sleeping beauties fancied taking his boots, they would have to reach up over his head to untie them. And he'd be ready for them! Equally, he placed his rucksack under the pillow for safety's sake.

He removed his raincoat and decided to use it as a blanket. The truth was, after going to the hospital, he had no idea what his next move would be. In the following days all hell would break loose, but in what shape or form was still very much unknown. One thing was for certain as far as Sonny was concerned. He was ready.

It was just past midnight. He would wake at 4.00am.

Patch had taught him how to set his internal clock.

Sonny's sleep was restless at best. His mind flooded with the thoughts of the savage beating Rhian had gone through. The more the thoughts whirled around his head, the more the rage consumed him.

At exactly 4.00am he pulled the coat away, reached up and untied the laces of his boots fastened to the headboard, and put them on while still sat on the bed. He silently swung his legs off the bed and checked the room. The other occupants were still fast asleep. As far as he was aware they had no idea that he had joined them four hours earlier

He rubbed his hands over his face in an attempt to get the fuzziness of sleep out of his head, deeply inhaling and exhaling the stale bedroom air. Quietly grabbing his rucksack and coat he made his way to the washroom. It was clean and smelled of bleach. It was tiled in hospital white from floor to ceiling. There were two cubicle toilets, two showers and two wash basins. After using the toilet, he stood in front of one of the wash basins tucking his rucksack underneath, put the plug in and filled it with cold water. A mirror was fitted to the wall over the basin and he stared deeply at his own reflection. He hadn't been from the safety of the barn for twenty-four hours yet, but he already looked tired and strained. The beanie had flattened his hair and made it look in need of a wash, his stubble made his face look dark and menacing. But his eyes were still calm and determined.

He splashed his face and hair vigorously with the cold water, instantly washing the tiredness away. A pile of mixed, clean towels were stacked in a nearby cupboard. He took one and dried himself off, running his hands through his hair to shape it up best he could. After putting on and zipping up his coat, he took another look at himself in the mirror, deciding to keep the beanie in his pocket and let his hair dry naturally.

He fitted the rucksack across his shoulders, slipped out of the washroom, and across the sleeping area without a sound. The door was slightly ajar, so with his training, he eased it open without a sound. Sylvie was reading a paperback novel, an empty teacup in front of her.

'Joseph, are you leaving us? Can you not sleep, son?' she asked, slightly taken aback.

'Not very well, Sylvie, so I thought I might as well crack on early and get out of the city and on my way before the morning chaos springs to life,' Sonny replied, with a ready prepared reason for his early departure.

Sylvie again offered him a look that said she wasn't born yesterday, but wasn't going to push him on his reasons.

'Well you take care, my boy. May God bless and guide you.' She shot up from the desk and made her way to the door, unlocking and opening it for Sonny to leave. Sonny looked into the old lady's kind face and thought about the next few days. What he was about to do certainly wasn't going to come with God's blessing and guidance, that's for sure.

'Thank you,' he replied and stepped out into the dark, cold morning.

Leaving absolutely nothing to chance, and after studying the city map, Sonny made his way to the Heath Hospital using the quietest roads possible. It was just before 5.00am and still dark when he arrived. From a good distance away, he studied the front entrance. Apart from a few cars parked sporadically the car park was relatively empty. There was no white van, but after a quick scout of the area Sonny spotted that it was parked on the corner of a street opposite, with a near perfect view of the front entrance of the hospital. Risking a quick look with his binoculars, Sonny could see one man sat in the driving seat, very much awake and alert.

Taking a long circuitous route, he made his way to the rear of the hospital, getting there for precisely 6.00am. There was no vehicle entrance. The rear of the hospital was surrounded by a six-foot privet hedge. All vehicles had to come through the front of the hospital and everyone who worked there had a pass card that would get them through the barrier at the side of the hospital.

After checking that the street was empty, Sonny managed to force himself through the privet hedge and into the rear car park. He found a good hiding place in a copse of topiary trimmed display bushes and settled himself in.

Once he was satisfied that he couldn't be seen, he took a one-hundred-and-eighty-degree survey of his position.

Soon, a blue Mini headed in the direction of the car park, coming to a stop about fifty yards from his hiding place. With the olive green outdoor clothing and covert training, he was invisible from sight. Sonny didn't move an inch for the next twenty minutes. He sat and listened, tuning in and out of sounds or movements that may, or may not, have brought danger his way. When he was absolutely satisfied that Holly had not been followed, he took one final look at the area, including the windows of the hospital that overlooked the car park. He rose from his hiding place and strode purposefully and confidently to the Mini. He opened the passenger door and folded down the seat, so he could throw his rucksack onto the back seat. Folding the seat back into position, he climbed into the small vehicle.

Holly looked remarkably calm, considering the risk she was about to take. He remembered her from school. She was part of a Rhian's large group of close friends. Holly launched straight into her plan and handed Sonny a blue male nurse's tunic. He took off his coat and pullover and put it on. She then took a couple of pens from the glove compartment and fixed them into the breast pocket for a more genuine look, even though Sonny was wearing outdoor walking trousers and boots. She also handed him a clipboard with some A4 sheets of out-of-date graphs and files.

'OK, we'll go in through the staff entrance over there.' Holly pointed to a small door with a keypad on the wall.

'We'll take the lift to the intensive care ward on the second floor. Rhian is in room one, the first door on the right as we go into the ward. Walk and act naturally, as if you know exactly where you are and where you are going.' Sonny nodded that he understood his instructions.

'Staff handover is between half six and half seven, so nearly all staff going off shift and coming on will be in the meeting room at the far end of the ward. Hopefully there will be hardly anyone around.'

Holly then looked seriously at Sonny.

'Her condition is stable, but she is still unconscious. You won't have long. You can talk to her. She will hear you.'

Sonny nodded. Holly seemed a lot more grown up than he remembered.

'OK, you ready?' she asked.

Sonny took a deep breath and nodded again. 'Yes, let's go.'

They both climbed out of the vehicle. Holly locked her door, but told Sonny to leave his side unlocked, so he could pick up his things afterwards.

Then they both strode confidently to the staff entrance door and Holly punched in the code for them to get inside. 'There isn't a code to leave the building, just press the green button and the door will open,' said Holly.

There was a loud ping as they entered the foyer, and the lift door opened and a weary looking nurse stared back at them. Sonny froze for a second, before he raised a confident smile at the nurse and held the door open for her to leave the building. She smiled back and gave him a quick, 'Thank you,' as she left.

They entered the lift and Holly pressed the first-floor button and the doors closed quickly.

'You'll have no more than five minutes, OK. When I tell you it's time, it's time. If you get discovered I will have to disappear. You see, I don't work on this ward and have no business being here.'

Sonny grabbed Holly by the hand. 'I understand, Holly, and thank you. I am really grateful for your help,' he replied.

The lift pinged as it quickly reached the first floor. It slid open with a wheeze. The corridor was deserted and, after no more than fifteen paces of Sonny holding the clipboard confidently, they were at intensive care room one. Holly nodded to him and, without hesitation, Sonny slipped quietly into the room.

Sonny felt his heart break at the sight that met his eyes. His Rhian, his beautiful Rhian. Both her eyes were black and squeezed tight shut, due to the bruising and swelling. Her head was swathed in bandages and there was strapping holding her jaw tightly shut. Her left arm was heavily plastered from fingers to shoulder, and her right leg plastered up to the thigh. She was hooked up to all kinds of beeping machines.

A standard hospital chair was positioned next to the bed, and Sonny quickly made use of it before his legs gave way. He never took his eyes away from his girlfriend. His mind flashed back to the last time they had met in Birmingham and his eyes filled with tears.

He took Rhian's right hand and pressed her fingers against his cheek and kissed her palm.

'It'll be over soon enough, Rhi,' he whispered. 'And I promise that when it is all done Byron will be gone forever.'

The door opened slightly, and Holly stepped into the shadows.

'That's it, Sonny, you've got to go. It's getting a bit busy now. Someone might want to check her stats.'

Sonny nodded in compliance. *Had that really been five minutes?* He looked back at Rhian, his first love; his only love! He needed her to know that he'd been to see her, so he took the hair band from his wrist and looped it twice around the wedding finger on her right hand – a future proposal gesture.

He kissed her palm and gently laid her hand down on the bed and made his way to the door. Clipboard in hand, he stepped back into the hallway to join Holly, and they both strode confidently out of the ward. The lift was open so they quickly got inside.

'I can take you to the ground floor, but you'll have to leave the building alone. My shift starts soon,' said Holly. 'I do wish you luck, Sonny. Just don't get yourself hurt, OK.'

The lift pinged, and Sonny hugged Holly. He thanked her again for what she had done and the risk that she had taken.

As soon as the lift door opened, he strode confidently across towards the door and hit the green button. He did not give the hospital a backwards glance, just walked towards the Mini, opened the passenger seat and took off the tunic. It was nearly 7.00am and starting to get light. He put his pullover and coat back on, and sat back in the seat to gather his thoughts.

His sadness, guilt and tears had been replaced by an overwhelming thirst for vengeance, but the newly trained soldier in him knew he needed to harness those feelings. And execute his plans with precision and cunning.

Once he made his first move, the war was on.

CHAPTER TWENTY-TWO
Killed or Killer

Once Sonny was back on the street he felt more vulnerable without the comfort of the dark, so zipped his coat all the way up and pulled the beanie down tight on his head.

On his way to the hospital he had come across a small woodland area with a derelict outbuilding, so decided to head back there. It took him about a half an hour. After he had eaten some of the dried food he had packed, he removed a smaller bag from his rucksack and filled it with the essentials he would need.

He then dropped the rucksack into a heavy duty black bin bag and quickly dug a hole just big enough to drop it in. He covered it over with dead foliage for easy retrieval later. He slung the smaller bag over his shoulder and made his way back to the road.

It was coming up to 9.00am and the city was very much alive. He now felt reasonably safe enough to watch the white van from behind. Its occupant was still staring ahead at the entrance. Sonny had formulated a plan, but it very much depended on one thing. The van driver had to leave the vehicle at some point for no more than a few minutes. Patch had taught Sonny that when conducting a long surveillance of a target, especially if they are in a vehicle, one of three things will make them leave that vehicle at some time: discomfort, food or toilet needs.

*

Jay Fowler may have given the appearance of concentration, but his mind was actually somewhere else – the hot young bird that was giving him the come on last night. *What was her name?* Susie Rees. She was nineteen years old; all mini skirt and cleavage. Jay was thirty-three and lived with Sally and their three kids, but this didn't enter his mind. He kept himself fit and the birds always said how good looking he was. *I'll be cracking onto young Susie the first chance I get, no mistake*, he thought.

He had only managed three hours sleep before 'volunteering' to do this job. It was a relief to be away from Sally. She had been giving him a hard time lately about his wandering eye, and a good slap across the head shut her up. He needed his beauty sleep for fuck sake.

He had an ulterior motive for helping to hunt down young Sonny. Alf Wilton had sacked him for his unnecessary violent tendencies. It usually went down like this: if a man took offence at Jay chatting up his wife or girlfriend, he would knock the living daylights out of him, and sometimes the wife or girlfriend as well if he felt they asked for it.

He had been given plenty of warnings, but it always fell on deaf ears. Then, Alf showed up at the club. Jay had been chatting up the young girls and putting his weight around, and Alf unceremoniously sacked him on the spot. The bastard! He was just doing his job.

Byron had taken him back on the quiet and let him in on what he had planned, and Jay loved it. He had been one of the trusted few that had dumped Alf's body down the mine shaft. The thought of killing Sonny appealed to him immensely. But he had to admit that surveillance was kind of boring.

He had been sitting there since 5.00am and wouldn't be relieved until 5.00pm, when Rod Collins would take over.

Everyone knew that Rod hated Byron. All except Byron! And because he worked the nightshift, Rod seemed to escape any retribution. He was very much a loner and working nights seemed to suit him well. On his own all night, sleep on his own all day. He would talk freely about how he enjoyed working for Alf. He would say the old boss trusted him and treated him well, and Byron wouldn't even acknowledge him most of the time. But, nobody in Byron's crew wanted to work nightshifts so, for some reason, peopled turned a blind eye to his disloyal comments.

Jay was getting hungry and his legs were stiffening up. He had been getting out and standing in front of the van to stretch his legs, while still keeping watch on the hospital, and taking a leak in the alley next to the van behind the wheelie bin. It was nearly 10.00am and, nipping away for a few minutes to get something to eat and drink, was becoming more than a fleeting temptation. It hadn't occurred to bring a packed lunch. That was for school kids.

Rod had moved the van out of the hospital car park last night when an attendant started having a go. Also, if the van stayed in the same place for more than twenty-four hours it would probably attract attention, which Jay thought was fair enough.

It was parked in an ideal place now though. No parking limits and there was a phone box right across the road if he had to call Byron or Pete, but there was also a transport café about fifty yards down the street, and the smell of bacon had been driving Jay nuts for the last hour or so.

He made the decision to run to the café, get them to knock up a quick takeaway sausage and bacon sandwich and cup of tea. He would be gone no more than five minutes and he could dump any evidence in the wheelie bin. If Rod asked he would tell him he toughed it out.

He stood in front of the van taking in a good look of the car park, before he set off at a speed towards the café.

*

Sonny had been patiently watching the van for over an hour from his safe vantage point. Earlier in the morning he had done a loop around a few streets to have a look at things from behind, and noted the shops including the café.

He recognised the man from the day his grandfather was murdered. Right now, he could see him standing in front of the van. Sonny correctly anticipated that he was about to take off somewhere – and then it all happened, quickly.

The man turned and started to head down the street towards the café. Sonny pulled the beanie from his head, leapt away from his safe spot and sprinted towards the van, getting there just at the time he anticipated the man would enter the café.

He quickly checked that there was no one around, then opened his bag, took out the sliding tool and popped the lock on the passenger side in no more than two seconds. Just like he had been shown, many times. He checked that there was nothing on the passenger seat and nothing in the footwell. He then closed the door and casually walked across the road and into the phone box. He pulled a pair of combat gloves out of his bag. They had been adapted by Patch and a steel sleeve had been stitched into the little finger of each glove, and an inch-wide steel plate along the outside of the hand. He pulled the gloves on, then watched and waited. He felt remarkably calm.

Two or three minutes passed before the man reappeared. Sonny could see he was carrying a well wrapped sandwich and a polystyrene cup. He hoped that the man would want to eat his breakfast in the relative warmth and comfort of the van, but it wouldn't really matter either way. He would be getting back into the van eventually, before or after his breakfast.

As he arrived the man did a quick scan of the car park. Satisfied that there had been no outstanding occurrences while he had been gone he opened the driver's side door, leaned in to put the hot cup of tea in the holder near the gear stick and the sandwich on top of the dashboard. He then settled back in the driver's seat. Sonny allowed the man a couple of seconds to tear open his sandwich – the time he needed to leave the phone box and take the already counted five strides to the passenger side of the van. He swung the door open and threw himself into the passenger seat.

Patch had so many times talked about the 'hunted' turning the tables and becoming the 'hunter'. With a few precious seconds gained, the one who *was* the hunter displays confusion, shock, outrage, and even fear, as he tried to address what was happening.

This is the time to strike.

Do not display any smugness to your enemy that the tables have been turned. Do the deed and get out. The man most definitely displayed confusion and shock at the sudden intrusion. He had already taken a bite out of his sandwich when the first heavy karate chop smashed into and caved in his nose. His head whipped back exposing his throat and the four karate chops, delivered with devastating force to the Adams apple, completely obliterated his windpipe. His body went immediately into panic mode. Any fight that he had in him had been instantly tempered. He dropped the sandwich onto his lap and his hands went to his throat. The man looked directly at Sonny with unimaginable panic. A choking, gurgling noise started to come from his mouth and the pieces of half chewed sandwich spewed onto his jacket. Then the fitting started. First with his legs, both kicking out indiscriminately at the pedals of the van. Then, as the brain went into full shock the man's hands dropped from his throat to his side and his body started to convulse uncontrollably.

Sonny sat transfixed in the passenger seat. He was shocked at having to witness the death of a man sitting right next to him, but he also knew this man was part of a gang that were intent on killing him.

The picture of Rhian, lying in the hospital was still imprinted in his mind. His grandfather shot in the face, and his grandmother callously murdered. So, he would feel no remorse or regret. This was the start.

The man's body had stopped thrashing around in the vehicle and was now just twitching slightly as the last seconds of life left. Sonny grabbed hold of the man's head and pulled it down onto his lap, covering the nose and mouth to finish the job off completely.

A woman pushing a crying child in a pram and another crying child in tow went by, but paid absolutely no attention to the two occupants of the van.

Sonny pushed the now very dead man back into a sitting position and reached over and triggered the lever to recline the driver's seat. He then climbed over his own seat into the rear of the van and dragged the body into the back, covering it with a blanket that had been rolled up there.

He climbed back into the driver's seat and put it back into the upright position. He had kept gloves on at all times, so there were no fingerprints and he had not been seen by any one. He was about to leave the van when he noticed the Post-It note stuck to the dashboard. *'Bloody cold last night so I've left my blanket in the back for tonight. See you at 5'.* Sonny checked his watch. Half past ten, he had a good head start.

CHAPTER TWENTY-THREE
The Heat is On

To say there was a tense and hostile atmosphere in the scrapyard office would have been an understatement. The three occupants were all arguing at the same time. The most hostile conflict was between DC Sharpe and Byron, sitting behind the office desk with the detective stood in front. Pete Sawyer, sat in an old armchair away to one side, for his part was desperately trying to calm the situation, trying to avoid Byron stabbing or shooting the old detective.

'You're more than fucking lucky that there isn't a murder investigation going on, Byron. What the fuck did you think you were fucking doing?'

Sharpe pointed an accusing finger at Byron, who seemed to be enjoying himself and doing his best to maintain his, 'I can't believe you'd think I would do such a thing' look on his face.

'How many fucking times have I got to tell you, Sharpie, it wasn't me? I left the club and was at Natalie's, you know that nasty little bird at the Vauxhall? She was up for it, I can tell you; loved the violent stuff!' He looked at Pete with a big grin on his face.

'Wahey!' shouted Pete, in support of his best friend. This

was despite being the person who had cleaned Byron up and had given him a change of clothes, after he had been knocked out of bed at half past three on the Sunday morning and been told the actual story.

Even though he had known Byron nearly all his life, the way his friend could talk about the sometimes horrible and shockingly violent incidents with total nonchalance and calm, could still shock him. It would shock the hardest of men. As if it was totally normal to beat a young woman half to death in a dark alley, and then leave her there to almost freeze to death. This scared Pete, but he was in too deep to ever think about getting away from him, not that he wanted or intended to. The money and lifestyle was just too good, and it afforded the time and contacts for him to indulge in the more exotic stuff.

'Well the heat is very much on, my friend.' The tired looking detective carried on. 'That poor girl's beating has stirred emotions in officers with daughters the same age. I'll do my best to detract the attention away from you, but I'm making no promises.'

'How many fucking times have I got to tell him it wasn't me, Pete?' Byron opened a drawer in the desk and pulled out an envelope stuffed with five thousand pounds in used notes. He tossed the envelope onto the desk in DC Sharpe's direction.

'Now *you* listen up, DC fucking Sharpe, I will say this just the once. Firstly, I'm not your fucking friend. Secondly, you've been taking a lot of money from me, so go and fucking earn it. And thirdly, if I *do* get fucking pulled for this you can forget about your police pension. That, I promise you, you dirty corrupt bastard, do you understand?'

Byron pointed towards the office door to let the detective know in no uncertain terms that this conversation was well and truly over. DC Sharpe picked up the envelope and tucked it in the inside pocket of his coat. Without saying another word, the detective turned and left the office.

Once he had gone , Byron turned on the swivel chair to his best friend, his hands hooked behind his head.

'The thing is, fella, you know what I'm like once I start. The red mist comes down and I can't stop.' He was actually smiling at his best friend as if to extract some kind of justification for what he had done.

'I only planned on giving her a couple of slaps, an overnight stay in the hospital, that was it. Flush the little fucker out, y'know what I mean. But she fucking wound me up in the club. I'm telling you now, Pete, she fucking knows where he is. I fucking well know it. And I am positive that her lying in the hospital is going to make him show his face sooner or later.'

Pete sat forward in the chair. His words were quiet, as if he didn't want anyone else to hear, even though the office was empty apart from the two of them.

'You know Sharpie's right though. She could've fucking died out there, and there would've been an entire world of shit round here if she had, as if it isn't bad enough.'

'Well I tell you what, old pal, I got a right old stiffie while I was slapping her about. So, she's lucky she's not suffering from injuries of a sexual nature because believe me, it crossed my fucking mind.' He winked at Pete, who sat totally dumbfounded at his friend's confession. Pete then thought about his own dalliances with his *young* girls, and how much he enjoyed threatening control during those games. This reminded him to phone his contact in Newport later and see if something could be arranged. He was feeling that urge again.

Byron grabbed at a set of keys lying on the desk and locked the drawers. He tossed them in the air a couple of times, before pocketing them and looking at his watch. It was 5.50pm and already dark outside. Standing, he rubbed the back of his neck. He pulled the leather jacket from the back of the chair and shrugged it onto his huge frame.

'Right, let's get the fuck outta here. I'm off home for a bite to eat and a shower. I'll meet you in the Vauxhall, about eight o'clock. We'll have a couple in there and see what happens.'

Pete was about to get up when the door of the office flew open and Rod Collins walked straight in. He was wide-eyed, ashen white and very agitated.

'What the fucking hell are you doing here?' Byron asked him. 'Tell me you've seen him or tell me you know where he is. Or I'm gonna kick you around the yard for half a fucking hour.' He leaned forward putting his fists onto the desk. He wasn't sure whether he was angry or excited as he waited for the answer from the nervous looking older man.

Rod spoke slowly and concisely. He wanted to avoid confusion. If Byron didn't understand what he was about to say, he would be the first man in the line of fire. 'The van is parked at the back of the yard next to the crusher. I've told everyone out there not to go near it.' Byron didn't move but continued to lean over the desk, looking confused and impatient.

'Guv, Jay's dead and he's in the back of the van.'

Byron was momentarily dumbstruck. He stared hard at the man in front of him. He had known Rod for a long time, but he always kept himself to himself. No wife or girlfriend. Liked his fishing. He even lived on a boat, out on Cardiff harbour.

Byron had always found him harmless and trustworthy enough. He was happy doing night shifts on lookout or night watchman. A brass-monkey type: see, hear and speak nothing. Did the job, took the money and buggered off back to his boat

Rod carried on, 'When I turned up for my shift the van was empty and locked, but I had my spare keys with me. It fucking smelled of piss and Ray was dead in the back. It looks like he's had his throat smashed in.' He paused to make sure this was being taken in.

'There was a sandwich and takeaway mug all mashed up in the footwell. The stupid idiot must have left the van for some grub. And bam! He's pushing up the daisies.'

Byron looked at Rod as if he had just arrived in his office on a spaceship while he struggled to digest the facts. He stood up and folded his arms across his chest. 'Hang on a fucking minute here, Rod. Jay is one of the hardest and nastiest bouncers I have *ever* met. Are you telling me that eighteen-year-old, still wet behind the fucking ears, Sonny Wilton – because that's what I'm guessing here – has jumped in the van while he's eating

a sandwich and beat him to fucking death?'

Rod shrugged his shoulders. 'Look, Byron, the man I was supposed to be taking over from is dead, so excuse me for feeling rather fucking nervous. I thought it best to get back here, so we can work out what to do.'

Byron looked incredulously at Pete. 'Couldn't be him, could it, Pete?'

Pete Sawyer was equally dumbfounded. Speechless, in fact. All he could do was open his arms and shrug his shoulders.

Byron carried on, 'What, has he been ninja training for the last six fucking months or what?' He took the office keys out of his jacket and opened the desk drawer. He counted out five hundred pounds from a massive wad of notes, shut the drawer and walked over to where a very nervous Rod stood. He slapped him on the shoulder and stuffed the money in his hand.

'Get yourself off, fella, and not a fucking word, OK.' 'Will do, I fancy some fishing up north anyway.'

Byron slapped Rob on the back and pushed him out of the door.

'Was that wise, boss?' asked Pete. 'He'll tell every fucker you know.'

Byron smiled. 'Not Rob, he's always been loyal.'

'To Alf Wilton maybe! Are you fucking blind? He hates you. Never stops going on about it.'

Byron sat back in his chair and folded his arms behind his head. 'Really? You think you know someone.' He opened the drawer to reveal a gun. 'Back of the head, Pete.' He tossed the gun at his loyal friend. 'And get my fucking money back!' He stood up. 'Right, let's sort out this bloody mess.'

Byron opened the office door and called out to Saville, his foreman in the scrapyard, and one of his inner circle of trusted gang members. Saville entered the office stinking of engine oil in his boiler suit. 'All right, By. White van is it?' he correctly guessed.

Byron was sitting back at the desk. 'Aye, strip all the wiring, get the wheels off and engine out. Put it through the crusher and hose it down. Then get it on the next load of scrap bales to the steel works for melting, OK. Good man.' He nodded and winked at the scrap worker.

Saville nodded his understanding and left the office. It wasn't the first time he had made a body disappear and probably wouldn't be the last. Say nothing and do as you're told.

Once Saville had left, Byron rested an elbow on the desk and rubbed the stubble on his chin.

'Well, well, who'd have thought it, Pete?'

'Sonny Wilton… murderer, we'd better lock all our doors to keep ourselves safe.' He looked at Pete with a huge grin on his face. Unlike Byron, Pete did, however, feel a little nervous and uncomfortable at the turn of events. Jay was a fucking evil bastard, so if Sonny killed him what did that mean for the rest of them?

'So, what now? We still don't know where he is.' Byron got up from his seat and walked to the window overlooking the yard. Saville had already got to work on the white van, the wheels were off and he was undoing the engine mounting bolts.

'No, but we know he's coming, Pete old pal. We know he's coming, and when he shows up, we'll be fucking ready. Oh, in the meantime I need you to go around to Jay's place and tell Sally that he's fucked off to Spain on the timeshare scams. She won't give a fuck; he's been slapping her around for years. Tell her I'll drop a wad around for her.'

Pete looked across at his friend, who was sitting back in the office chair with his fingers locked. He had a real uneasy feeling in the pit of his stomach. This was not going to go well.

CHAPTER TWENTY-FOUR
Food Glorious Food

Sonny had decided against using public transport to get to Mynydd Du. He didn't want to risk being recognised. Once outside the city he avoided the road altogether, using his map and compass to navigate the countryside.

What have I done? Sonny thought. *I've killed a man in cold blood.* He hated watching the man die before his eyes, but it was a necessary evil – an eye for an eye. Sonny had spent hours discussing the ethics of murder with Patch, but ultimately they had both come to the same conclusion – it was necessary! These men, if they found him, wouldn't hesitate to put a bullet in the back of his head. He couldn't live in the shadows forever, especially with Rhian lying in hospital. He had no choice; he had to strike first!

It took nearly five hours until he reached familiar surroundings. The sun was setting, so he made for a densely wooded area that he knew well. Once satisfied that he was completely alone, he set about making a hideout, using felled branches and piling up leaves for cover. It took about ninety minutes to build, and by the time he was finished it was dark, with just the light of the moon illuminating the ground. He also dug another hole about twenty yards away to stash his rucksack.

He collapsed to the ground with exhaustion. *Time to eat and rest for a few hours*, he thought. The best decisions are made with a rested mind and a full stomach. He had brought enough dried food to last a day or so and, if his memory served him correctly, there was a spring not far away to get clean water.

He decided against lighting a fire. The dead body in the van would have been discovered by now and, it stood to reason, that Byron's men would be out looking for him.

He sat outside the hideout and rummaged in his rucksack for food. He quickly wolfed down some raw carrots, a large packet of nuts and raisins, and a thick slice of fruit loaf. At 6.30pm he set his watch alarm for midnight. After unrolling a thin camping mattress and sleeping bag, he crawled into the hideout, shuffling around to make himself comfortable.

Surprisingly he was asleep quite quickly.

He woke before midnight and crawled out of the hideout. After a few stretches, he made his way through the darkness to the spring. Stripping to the waist, he swilled his face and hair with the ice cold water, and filled one of his water bottles. He then changed into his black trousers and fleece, grabbed his lock picking kit, a small cosh and a pair of gloves, and stashed the rest of his belongings in his rucksack.

With his beanie hat pulled tightly over his head, he made his way through the dew-soaked fields to the village. He was nervous, but considered this to be a safe way to feel, all things considered.

It took nearly an hour to get to his intended concealed spot. In the distance he could see *Hughes News and Groceries*. Next to this was his primary school. It felt weird to be here at night. He'd only ever seen the school during the day. Swiftly he climbed the railing and jumped into the playground.

At first he was surprised that nobody seemed to be watching from the shop. Then, after moving further along, he could clearly see a car parked on the corner of the street opposite. It appeared to be watching Rhian's family house instead. *Keeping an eye on Arthur are you, Byron?* thought Sonny. *Big mistake!*

Using his binoculars, Sonny deduced that there was a Yale lock on the shop door. *No problem,* he thought. At least it would be easy to pick the lock. He knew that the alarm was a standard key on/off type. He was sure that Rhian had told him the code once, but he couldn't remember it.

After fifteen minutes surveillance, he climbed the school railings again and dropped down into the street. He didn't stop to look around; he was satisfied that there was no one to see him, including the men in the car. He was already holding the picks he needed, and was in front of shop door in seconds. His hands were shaking, and he almost dropped the picks on the floor. He paused for a second, took a deep breath, and had the door open in no time.

Slipping inside the shop, he let his eyes adjust to the light from the fridge. The alarm started beeping its usual sixty second countdown. Despite spending time with Rhian in the shop, he had never actually switched the alarm on or off. This worried him a bit. What if he didn't do it in time? He slid in the two picks he had selected, found the barrel slots, and turned the switch. Even though he had done this countless times before with Patch, the relief he felt when the alarm switched off was palpable.

Hiding in the shadows, he looked out of the shop

window. Rhian's house was too far away to see but, the fact that there was no movement told him that everything was good so far. He slowly edged along the wall to the counter, and picked up the phone, dialling Mr Hughes' home number. It was answered on the second ring.

There was a confused and questioning, 'Hello?'

'Mr Hughes, I mean, Arthur. It's Sonny. I'm in the shop. I'm letting you know now, so you don't get a shock in the morning and give me away. I can see you're being watched, very closely.'

'What? Sonny? Oh, I know. They've been around since Sunday. How did you get in? Why didn't the alarm go off?'

'Oh, a few skills I've picked up recently. Can I please talk to you when you collect the papers? I need to know what's been going on and who's going where. Is that OK?'

'Course, Son, but I don't really know much, but if I can help you… Shall I come now?' he asked.

'Absolutely not,' Sonny said with authority. 'Keep your routine the same, no changes.'

'To be honest, Sonny, my routine has already been blown to bits with Rhian being in the hospital. Lets' see, I usually open up at five o'clock. I like to potter around a bit before the papers arrive.'

A car driving by illuminated the shop with its light.

Sonny quickly pulled himself behind a wall. 'Are you OK, Son?'

'Yes, Mr Hughes, Arth—'

'Holly phoned earlier today,' interrupted Arthur. 'Yes, I've been to see her,' said Sonny, as the light from the car faded.

'She'll be OK, Son. Us Hughes' are made of sterner stuff, you know.'

'And I'll be there when she's back, Arthur.'

'I hope so, Son. I really hope so. Right, I'll be there at five. Get some food down you. Help yourself to anything in the shop, except the box of Black Magic. I'm saving that for my wedding anniversary. Oh, there's an old armchair in the storeroom.'

'OK, thank you.' Sonny hung up the phone.

He went to the fridge and helped himself to a few pasties, sausage rolls, a pint of milk, and some sliced ham. He also picked up a bag of apples. *An apple a day*, he thought. Let's hope it did keep the doctor away. If everything went to plan, it wouldn't be *him* who'd need a doctor.

He quickly slipped into the storeroom, leaving the door ajar and adjusting the position of the chair, so he could see through into the shop. The armchair was surprisingly comfortable, and the storeroom warm and cosy. So, after he had eaten, he topped up his bag with food supplies, and then seized the opportunity to have a power nap.

He was startled awake by the sound of the shop door being opened and the lights being switched on. He could see Arthur locking the door and making his way to the alarm. For appearance sake, in case he was being watched, Arthur put the key into the alarm and turned it on, then back off again.

Sure enough, within sixty seconds the car that had watching the house pulled up opposite the shop.

'Morning, Son,' Arthur said loudly, although he did not look in the direction of the storeroom.

'Right, I'm going to sweep the shop floor. Got to keep up appearances, heh? I'll do my best to tell you everything I know. Don't worry about the car across the road. They can't see anything.'

'How many men are in Byron's closest circle?' asked Sonny. He opened his notebook to jot down short reminders for himself.

'I'm told he's got a dozen men doing his bidding. The rest are only loyal because they're scared of him. Some hate him, especially the ones that worked for your grandfather,' said Arthur as he pushed the broom around the shop.

'Is there a meeting place, a bar or office, where they meet up regular?'

Arthur stopped and rubbed his whiskered chin while he thought. 'Well there's The Den, about five or six of them go there every Wednesday night.'

'The Den?'

'Aye, remember the old café on Rose Street that belonged to Sybil Rigden?'

'Oh yeah, I remember.'

'That place closed down about six months ago. She's still got the lease on it, but her eldest boy, Anthony, who works for Byron has started using it. He's put a pool table in there, and every Wednesday Sybil cooks a big pot of curry and takes it round for them. They're usually in there until midnight playing cards, and then they bugger off to some other godforsaken place.'

Sonny was already forming a plan.

'My sister, Hazel, lives right across the road, and she's always complaining about the comings and goings. She gets very nervous now the kids are gone, and she lost her husband a couple of years ago.'

Sonny's plan was becoming even more appealing. He asked Arthur for a few addresses to help with the execution.

'What's happened to my grandfather's house?' he asked.

'All boarded up last time I walked up there. I heard Byron is trying to get ownership, but he can't get his hands on it until they get word from your grandparents.' He stopped sweeping and put his hands in his pockets, leaning broom handle up against the counter. 'Sorry, Son, I should have thought. That house and a lot of other things are rightfully yours, and I hope and pray that one day you will be able to take it all back.'

'Thank you, Arthur, so do I,' he replied. 'Now is there any chance we can have a chat with your sister?'

Without giving any detail of his real intentions, Sonny outlined his plan to Arthur. He needed to watch any activities going on at The Den from tonight through to late Wednesday night, from the very safe observation point of behind the net curtains of Arthur's sister's parlour. Arthur said that he would phone his sister later that morning.

The two goons were still parked outside when the newspaper delivery van pulled up twenty minutes later.

'I need to get out of here, Arthur,' said Sonny.

Arthur took an adjustable spanner from the counter drawer, put it on the floor and slid it into the storeroom with the sweeping brush. He also dropped a plastic bag containing ten pounds in coins. 'You'll need to keep in touch,' he said.

'Thanks, Arthur.'

'There's the small window in the toilet out the back. You should be able to squeeze through, but you'll have to take the burglar grille off first. I'll do the papers. That'll give those idiots something to watch.'

Sonny remembered that behind the shop was an alleyway that ran the length of the street. At the end was a fence. *Get over that and I will be in a farmer's field and back into the countryside*, he thought.

The grille came off easy enough and, in a couple of minutes, he was gone.

On the way back to his hideout he took a detour to a phone box he'd seen on the way. It was 8.30pm, and he guessed correctly that Patch would be back from his morning run on the five mile, showered and eating breakfast.

He gave Patch the full run down of everything that happened since Sunday, including the killing of Jay Fowler.

'Are you sure you're OK, Sonny? Killing a man can affect you,' said Patch.

'It's difficult, yes, but I've got to be strong. When Rhian gets better she needs to feel safe.'

'I know, I've trained you well, Kimosabe,' said Patch. Sonny smiled. He didn't expect Patch to be quoting *The Lone Ranger*.

Changing the subject, Sonny ran through his intended plan for Wednesday night. Patch was dubious, but could see what Sonny was trying to do.

'There will be a great deal of attention when it happens. With the authorities, I mean. You will have to be meticulously clean as far as they are concerned. No sightings, no clues,' he warned.

'I know, but he's only protected by about a dozen others. If I can reduce the strength around him, it puts me in a better position to get to him quicker,' Sonny reasoned.

'Then go for it. You'll need to get in there tonight, when the place is empty, to familiarise yourself with the layout. And if it all falls in place tomorrow, get it done.'

'I'll try and keep you posted. Bye.'

'Sonny, you know what you're doing, but be careful.' Sonny put the phone down, and headed straight back through the gate. He was soon back at the hideout. He washed himself down in the spring after retrieving his rucksack, and changed into a black tracksuit. After he had eaten, he rested through what was left of the day, thinking about his plan for the next twenty-four hours. He packed what he would need into the small kit bag, checking it several times until he was happy that he was fully prepared.

At 5.30pm it was already getting dark. He pulled on his black bomber jacket and made his way back to the phone box. At 6.00pm he called Arthur.

'Hello, Arthur, it's Sonny.'

'Hello, Son. You OK? My wife has just returned from the hospital. It looks like she's going to be OK. The doctors managed to coax her awake this morning.'

Sonny felt his heart rise at the news. 'What did she say?' asked Sonny.

'She doesn't remember anything about the attack, but the doctors say her amnesia is a defence mechanism. Aside from this, she's OK. Oh, and that bastard didn't rape her.'

Sonny's heart jumped a beat. 'Thank, fuck.'

'The wife says that she keeps touching the hairband wrapped around her finger. I take it that was you, Son?' 'I wanted her to know that I had been there,' Sonny confirmed.

'A very nice gesture, Son, and good for her morale. Now, I've spoken to my sister and she is more than happy for you to go around and watch The Den from her front room. The one thing she insists is that you come in through the back garden. I'm guessing that's what you had planned anyway. The houses are back to back with Blue Street, and there's an alleyway separating the back gardens, so it should be easy enough for you to get into hers. She's made sure the back gate is unlocked.'

Sonny thanked Arthur and was about to hang up, but he could sense that there was something else he wanted to say.

'Whatever you have planned for that murderous bastard, and all who stand with him, you have my family's blessing and a lot of other families as well. We wish you well, Son. Be safe.'

Sonny was grateful to hear those words, and the feeling grew inside him that what he was going to do was justified.

CHAPTER TWENTY-FIVE
The Den

Sonny made his way to Rose Street through the darkness, sticking to the shadows and back alleys whenever possible. He had taken a good look at the map before he had left the hideout and had counted the number of houses until he was a hundred percent positive that he was going through the correct and unlocked gate.

Once he had shut and locked the gate behind him, he moved into the darkness beside a small garden shed and studied the rear of the house, and the neighbouring houses either side. Arthur's sister, Hazel, sat in an armchair watching television, oblivious to Sonny's presence in her garden. The light was on in the living room, so there was no way she could see him. Satisfied, he made his way up the path and tapped lightly on the back door.

Hazel answered the door quickly and ushered him inside with an urgent wave. She was white-haired and had a kind face. She looked a lot older than Arthur.

'No need to explain your reasons, my boy. Arty has told me all I need to know.'

She made her way through the kitchen to the front room door. Sonny followed behind, unzipping his bomber jacket in the warm house. 'You are here to help, aren't you?' asked Hazel.

Sonny nodded.

'It was bad enough with the smell of greasy food wafting over here when Sybil was running the café, but now her boy, Anthony, and his mates have been using it for… erm, whatever! Well, all the neighbours are fed up. Mr Davies from a couple of doors down went across to complain about the noise and they broke his nose, poor man, and the police wouldn't do anything.'

Before Hazel opened the door to the front room Sonny asked if it was OK to turn out the hallway light. To her credit, the old lady tapped her nose in understanding, and flicked the switch into darkness.

They entered the room, closed the door and stood near the window. *The Den* was in darkness, directly across the street. The windows had been painted black and it looked like they were also boarded up from the inside. A small dark porch covered the entrance. It was obviously unoccupied and unused. This was confirmed by Hazel.

'Would you like a cup of tea or anything, dear?' Hazel asked.

'I'm OK, thank you, Hazel. I've brought some water. Never got the taste for tea. Thank you anyway.' He smiled at the old lady.

'OK, I'll leave you to it then, my love. My soap's about to start. I love my soaps. I usually go to bed around nine thirty. Don't worry about moving around. I won't hear a thing.'

That's good news, thought Sonny. He would be letting himself out later to familiarise himself with *The Den*. He didn't want Hazel to worry if there wasn't any need.

'I must say, I shall sleep even more soundly tonight knowing there is a big strong man keeping guard downstairs. I shan't disturb you from your observations again tonight, so I bid you goodnight, and shall see you in the morning for breakfast.'

Hazel made her way to the door and shut it quietly behind her, as if not to disturb anybody, leaving Sonny in the darkness.

Sonny grabbed a chair near the window and sat down for the long haul. He chose a dining chair instead of an armchair. The armchair looked far more comfortable, but he wanted to avoid the danger of falling asleep, at least for a few hours.

Nothing happened until about two hours in. Anthony Rigdon pulled up at around 10.00pm in a Land Rover with Ian Pyle, another one of Byron's crew. They both got out and pulled a case of beer each from the rear seats. They were laughing and joking as Anthony opened the door to the café. No lights went on after they went in, and they left less than a minute later. Sonny concluded that the card game was on for tomorrow and they were dropping off the drinks.

Sonny left it for another hour, and then thought that he wouldn't get a better time to look inside *The Den*. The pubs would be chucking out in thirty minutes, so he didn't have long.

He pulled on his beanie and left the house silently by the back door. He moved slowly up the side of the semi-detached house and, after checking the street was empty, moved swiftly across the street, into the alleyway on the opposite side of the road. *Hopefully there will be a back door*, he thought. He crept around the back, but the door had been heavily nailed shut and the window had been fortified with thick steel bars.

He moved silently down the side of the building to the front of *The Den*, right next to the porch. Swiftly, he looked at the lock and selected the picks that he would need to open the door. His adrenalin pumped hard through his body. He couldn't decide whether he was excited or scared. Or both.

After about thirty seconds he was sure that he had released the lock, but the door wouldn't open. Then, he realised that a handle had to be levered at the same time as the key was turned. He managed a smile at the schoolboy error, before he opened the door and disappeared inside, closing the door tight behind him.

It was pitch dark inside due to the blacked out and boarded up windows. He switched on the torch. He figured the torchlight couldn't be seen from outside, but just in case, kept the torch on a low light and the beam pointed at the floor.

The floor area of the café itself was a decent size. Three stacks of tables and chairs stood against the boarded-up windows. A pub size pool table was standing in the centre of the room, with two cues and two cases of lager on the baize. A large round table, with a couple of decks of cards on top, was close by. A large grubby settee and armchair against the wall was there to provide more seating, and a pretty good colour television was mounted on the wall opposite. An old dart board was also fixed to one wall with six darts stuck in it, and half decent music system with tapes sat on a café table near the entrance to the kitchen. This was the room that Sonny wanted to get a good look at. He mentally recorded how far ajar the door was open. He had to make sure the place was left exactly as he found it.

The kitchen was remarkably well kept. He put that down to Sybil Rigdon. After all, this had been her café for years, and she had been known for being quite fussy about keeping the hygiene standards high.

There were two gas cookers as opposed to a range, a large sink and drainer, a very large fridge with nothing but a couple of bottles of Coca-Cola and lemonade in, and an empty freezer. Shelving units held a variety of plates, bowls, cups and mugs.

There was no large pot of curry or any food at all in the kitchen. Sonny reasoned that if the card game was on for tomorrow night the food should arrive sometime during the day. It meant that he would have to sit at the window in Hazel's house until it arrived. It was going to be a long day.

Just at the moment that he had seen enough to satisfy his plan, the unmistakable sound of a diesel Land Rover pulled up sharply right outside *The Den*.

Sonny quickly switched off the torch and shoved it in the inside pocket of his bomber jacket. He put the kitchen door into the position it was when he came in. There was no way to get outside from the kitchen, and no time to try and find somewhere to hide in the large sparsely furnished area. He took the double-edged stiletto commando knife out of the bag. He would have to fight his way out of this fix if anyone came through that door.

The front door opened and Anthony Rigdon strode in, flicking the light on to the large room, with Ian Pyle close behind. He placed the four bottles of Southern Comfort and Smirnoff Vodka onto the pool table alongside the two cases of beer.

Anthony rubbed his hands together. 'I tell you what. It's getting fucking cold out there now, you know.'

'Tell me about it. And I forgot my coat,' Ian agreed, shrugging his shoulders a few times. Anthony stamped home Wednesday's arrangements.

'Right, my mam will bring the curry round tomorrow afternoon about two, and she'll put it on the hob to stew. Bloody lovely.'

Ian took a pool ball from one of the pockets and made a feeble attempt to bounce it off a cushion into another pocket. 'Johnny, Terry, Sam, oh and Barry are all up for it. Michael said he'd try to make it as well, as long as Byron doesn't want him doing something else.' He looked away from the pool table at his friend.

'He reckons Byron's losing the fucking plot with all this Sonny Wilton shit. Coked up all day lately, he says.' Anthony looked down at the floor and then back up.

He had to admit that Byron was scaring everyone these last few weeks.

'What can I say, mate, we all saw the pound signs. We all jumped in. It'll work itself out one way or the other. It'll have to because if it's got anything to do with Byron, there's no getting out.'

'Aye, I know. Terry wants to win back some of that fifty quid you took off him last time he was here,' Ian said, not looking at Anthony, having another attempt at the pool ball trick instead.

Anthony guffawed loudly. 'Aye, and I'll take another fifty quid off him while he's trying. Make sure you tell him to get six bags of chips on his way past tomorrow, and make sure they're fucking fresh. Come on, let's go. I'm fucking knackered.'

Ian stepped out into the street first, and after flicking the light off and, checking that he had his keys with him, Anthony pulled the door of *The Den* shut, and rattled it a couple of times to make sure it was locked. They both got into the Land Rover still giving the banter and took off into the night.

Sonny put the commando knife safely away and took a deep breath. This was all crucial information!

Checking his watch at just after midnight, he left *The Den* and retraced the steps he had taken an hour earlier. When he got back to Hazel's he locked the back door and quietly slipped back into the parlour. There was nothing more he could do, so he thought it best to take the opportunity of comfort, warmth and relative safety, and swapped the dining chair for the armchair, still positioning it to so he could see across to *The Den*, but he was going to get some well-earned sleep. He set his mental alarm clock for 6.00am.

It was raining heavily when he woke. He hoped that the rain would continue to fall all day. It would mean fewer people on the street in broad daylight. He would, however, have to make sure he took a towel to wipe away any wet footprints in *The Den*.

While he was swilling his face in the kitchen sink he could hear Hazel upstairs doing her morning rituals. She came down into the kitchen already dressed and smiled warmly at him.

'I don't want to know the details, but I hope your night in the parlour wasn't completely fruitless.'

She opened a kitchen cupboard and pulled out a large frying pan.

'I slept the sleep of the dead knowing that I had my personal security guard downstairs, so as a thank you, I am going to cook you a large breakfast. No arguments, take yourself back to your post and I shall bring it through to you when it's done.'

And she ushered him out of her kitchen.

Sonny went back into the front room and couldn't help but feel the irony that he was about to tuck into a full breakfast, when his intentions for that same evening also concerned a hearty meal. He swapped his seating arrangement back to the dining chair and carried on watching the front of *The Den*.

He wolfed down a huge cooked breakfast. He got the impression that Hazel was quite enjoying the goings on in her quiet little house, and that she was quite grateful for the company. She also informed him that she would be out of the house until around 5.00pm visiting, and gave him a key to the back door.

At just after 2.00pm the rain was still falling steadily as a Ford Fiesta pulled up outside *The Den*. A small, round woman wearing a headscarf, got out and ran quickly into the porch and opened the door wide. She then rushed back out to the car, opened up the tailgate and lifted out a very large and very full saucepan. The woman hastily carried it through the door and pushed the door shut with her backside.

Sybil Rigden carried the heavy saucepan containing the very tasty and still quite warm chicken and vegetable curry through to the kitchen. She placed it on top of one of the cookers. After taking off her headscarf, she took the plates from the shelves and stacked them on the worktop. From the drawers she removed the cutlery she needed and a serving spoon. She was very fussy about the order of her kitchen. She could never abide her lummox of a husband, or her kids, rummaging around the cupboards and drawers looking for things and untidying everything. So, she always made sure that everything needed was out on the worktop in plain sight.

She never bothered with beer glasses because her Anthony usually drank straight from the can. However, she did put out a dozen short glasses for the four large bottles of spirits that she noticed when she came in.

After lighting the gas hob and, turning it down to one, she gave the curry a good stir and rested the spoon on the drainer. She scribbled a note to 'switch off the gas ring' and sellotaped it to the eye level grill. She then made two trips to the pool table, each time carrying a case of beer. Busting open the cases, she stacked them up in the fridge.

Finally, she left the kitchen, leaving the door wide open, so the smell of her curry wafted through into the large room as it simmered. She took the bottles from the pool table and placed them in the middle of the round card table, and switched on the fan heater in the corner. While tying her headscarf back on, Sybil did a quick mental check that everything had been done. Anthony, and his mates, all chipped in a tidy lump for her to cook something up for them on Wednesday nights and, to be honest, she quite enjoyed doing it since she'd stopped running the café.

Satisfied that all was in order, she hurried out in the rain and got in her car. It was 2.45pm. She had some shopping to do before cooking her old man his tea. Then it was bingo with the girls for 7.00pm.

*

Sonny watched the woman drive away and, after waiting another thirty minutes, decided it was now or never. He checked his bag to make sure that he had everything he needed, and left the house exactly the same way he had the night before. The rain had eased off to a drizzle. This time, when he reached the alleyway across the other side of the road, he followed it right to the end and into Rose Street, about eight doors away from *The Den*. He walked down the street as calmly and nonchalantly as he could, until he reached the porch. A man was miserably walking his dog in the rain, but he didn't pay any attention to Sonny.

He quickly dived into the porch with the lock pick already in his hand, and was through the door and inside the building in seconds. As soon as he had shut the door, he pulled out an old towel. It looked like it hadn't been used for years. He had acquired it from the bottom of a huge pile in the back of Hazel's airing cupboard, and figured that she wouldn't even notice that it had gone. He threw it on the floor and stamped his boots dry the best he could.

The smell of the simmering curry from the kitchen had permeated the large room. Already familiar with the layout Sonny made his way straight to the kitchen.

The saucepan was simmering with enough curry to feed a dozen men, never mind six or seven. Out of his kit bag Sonny pulled out a smaller cloth bag containing approximately two hundred grams of death cap toadstools (Amanita phalloides). He remembered the warnings Patch had given him about them when he was getting his foraging lesson. He had collected a lot of them over the last few months, but when he had dried the moisture out they had condensed down to what he had in the bag with him now. He had studied and read about them at length, using the books that Patch had at the barn, and knew that no potency was lost when drying or freezing them.

Cruelly, they also smelt delicious when being cooked, although any aroma was going to be masked by the smell of this curry.

Sonny undid the knot on the bag. He figured that because there was a lot of curry, the whole of the bag could go in. Using the large spoon from the drainer he emptied and stirred the whole two hundred grams of deadly poisonous fungi into the saucepan.

He replaced the spoon in the exact spot that he had taken it from. If Sybil did return she wouldn't notice anything different. He didn't touch or do anything else. Backing out of the kitchen and heading to the door, he used the towel to wipe away any footprints that he had left. The window of the café door was frosted up and couldn't be used to check outside. He had to take the risk of slipping out and shutting it behind him, without being seen by anyone in the street.

But once he was out of the café, a quick look up and down the road told him that the coast was clear. He turned and walked away.

Sonny wanted to change his clothes, so he decided to head back to the hideout. He would have to be quick though. Hazel got home at 5.00pm, and she could help him identify everyone at the card game. He wasn't going to tell Hazel what was going on. The less she knew the better. It was safer that way.

Everything was how he had left it at the hideout, so after a quick look around he headed to the phone box to call Arthur. After reassuring Sonny that Rhian was in the clear and improving by the hour, the curiosity got too much for Arthur and he asked the young man what his plans were.

'If everything goes the way I hope tonight, Arthur, there will be panic throughout the Lewis ranks.'

'Well, be bloody careful, do you hear?' Arthur warned.

'Don't worry, it's already done. I've got to go now, bye.' Sonny hung up.

Arthur put down the phone with a heavy frown on his face. 'What the hell does he mean, it's already done?'

Sonny didn't foresee anything else happening that evening, apart from watching the arrivals of everyone at *The Den*, so he opted to stay in his black tracksuit. He did, however, seeing as it was getting dark, do a circuitous route of both the living spaces of Pete Sawyer and Byron Lewis for future reference.

Pete lived in a large flat above a car repair garage that legally belonged to Sonny's grandfather. It was almost a legitimate business when Alf owned it, aside from the odd ringer that passed through once in a while. A nice new car would go missing from a rental company. They would, of course, claim on their insurance. That motor would then gain new registration and a whole new identity from Alf's mechanics, and get sold on for a nice profit.

Now it was just used as a chop shop. MOT failures and road traffic accident right offs were botched up, cleaned down, given dodgy MOT certificates, and sold to some poor unsuspecting soul.

As well as the stone steps that led up to the front door of the flat, Sonny noted the metal fire escape stairs and entry door at the rear. *I can pop that no problem*, he thought.

Byron, on the other hand, seemed to move around a lot. He would stop over for a few nights here and there, always with a bird in tow. He liked the small hotels and motels around town, and had private rooms in nightclubs for obvious reasons. Arthur had given him the address of a house that everyone knew as his. He used it for all legal mail and correspondence.

Sonny still planned to have a look around both dwellings when the opportunity came. He made his way back to Hazel's just after 5.00pm, meticulously sticking to the safe route that he had found the night before. The house was in darkness, telling him that he had made it back before her. He let himself in through the back door, but didn't put any lights on. After all, a nosey neighbour could have seen Hazel walking up the street, and raised suspicions.

Sonny settled himself on the dining chair near the window as the old lady walked past. So, as not to scare or startle her, Sonny announced his presence in the front room. She immediately understood as to why he hadn't put any lights on.

After Hazel had made herself a cup of tea, Sonny asked her if she would mind sitting with him for a while. She was only too willing and quite excited to help.

First to arrive on foot at 6.00pm was the host, Anthony Rigdon, with his best friend, Ian Pyle, following about five minutes later. Johnny Hill and Terry Owens arrived at 6.15pm, parking a Ford Granada round the corner near the alley. Terry was carrying a large carrier bag from 'Hobbs Fish 'n' Chips'. They let themselves into the building, so Sonny guessed that Anthony had put the door on the latch. Five minutes after that, Barry Wilkins and Sam Crossley came swaggering up the street. Hazel had put names to them all, except Sam Crossley, but Sonny, of course, knew the fat bully.

He had jotted down the names of everyone and thought that was it, when a taxi pulled up and another man headed towards the door. He was dressed smartly in polished shoes, shirt and trousers with an expensive looking blazer. He was welcomed with a hug and back slap from Anthony Rigden before they went inside.

'That's Michael Lewis that is, Byron's younger brother, another nasty one that boy,' Hazel confidently informed Sonny.

'Oh, really. That's going to make things very interesting,' Sonny replied, trying to imagine what was going on right now inside the old café.

He had been reliably informed that Wednesday night at *The Den* was an all-male – Lewis crew member only – affair. No innocents would be involved in this night.

11.05pm and Anthony Rigdon sat back in the chair at the card table, smiling to himself as the others gathered their coats to leave. It had been a cracking few hours and the banter and piss take had been fast and furious. Everyone apart from Michael, who had never been a big drinker like his older brother, was pretty well watered.

Bob Marley had been giving it large for a few tapes, followed by a bit of UB40. They had got through a good few joints chilling out to the reggae tunes, and there were only about three cans of lager left in the fridge. The poker table had been kind to him, and he was a good eighty quid up again.

As for his mother's curry, that had been well and truly cleaned out. It went down a storm with the fresh cooked chips that Terry had insisted on getting. Michael, Sam and himself had paid three visits each to the trough, with fat Sam even cleaning the dregs from the saucepan and spoon. Even Ian had two platefuls and he would normally moan that curries gave him the shits. But it was no surprise really, his mam had run this café for years. One thing she knew was how to fill a man's belly, and all the lads were suckers for her curries.

The pre-booked taxi had just pulled off with Michael in it, and there was only Anthony and Ian left. Ian had put his coat on, but had dropped off to sleep in the old armchair.

Anthony got up from the card table, turned off the fan heater and pulled on his own coat. He went over to the armchair and hauled Ian up.

'C'mon, piss head, time to get outta here.'

'Aye, I'm good. Well, I'm not good actually, Bro. I feel a bit sick to be honest,' Ian confessed.

'Well that's because you're a thirsty bastard, especially when it comes to vodka. Now get the fuck outside, you're not puking up in here. My mother draws the line at cleaning up puke. Plates, glasses, cans and pots, aye. Puke, no.'

He manoeuvred his mate to the door and out into the fresh air. Going back into the café to turn out the light, he slammed the door shut as he left. The pair then started the half mile drunken trudge back home. They only lived four doors down from each other. Ian with his girlfriend, Shelley, of eight years, and Anthony, still with his parents. Anthony had a bird on the high street. She had been hammering him about moving in with her for ages, but it was a bit noisy at night, and she couldn't cook as good as his mam.

He got Ian to his front door and gave it a knock. Shelley answered after a minute or so in her dressing gown. She gave Anthony a disapproving tut and then tugged her man through the front door by the arm. Anthony also got a sarcastic smile from Shelley as she shut the door on him.

He didn't look too good at all Anthony thought, and laughed to himself as he put the key into his parents' front door. Rubbing his own stomach, he was beginning to think that his mam's curry was working its magic there as well.

Sonny had observed each man as they left *The Den*. Of course, he had no way of knowing who had eaten the poisoned curry, or how much they had eaten, but over the next few days he would certainly find out. The bush telegraph was the bullhorn of all news, once the drums started beating.

He wrote a note to Hazel, who had taken her pill and gone up to bed nearly three hours ago. He bid her goodbye and thanked her for letting him stay and reminded the old lady that no one apart from her brother, Arthur, knew that he had been there to stay. So, she was quite safe as long as it stayed that way.

He decided to stay at the hideout for the next few days. Because when this blew up, as it was bound to do very quickly, the opportunity to cut the snakes head off may come sooner, rather than later. He wanted to be ready.

CHAPTER TWENTY-SIX
Fall Out

Sybil Rigden was out of the house by 7.00am. Her husband had left for work at the foundry two hours earlier. She was sure she had heard Anthony getting up a few times during the night. Over indulgence she suspected. She was at The Den by 7.15am, straight into the kitchen, and was more than pleased to see her curry had been well and truly polished off. She wasn't keen on spicy food herself – it upset her system.

The large sink in the kitchen was filled with soapy water, and all plates, glasses, cutlery and ash trays were gathered up, washed clean, dried and put away. The work tops were wiped down with a bleached cloth, and all the rubbish was dropped on the pavement outside.

The card table was wiped down with a damp cloth. She sprayed nearly half a tin of air freshener around the room, and then quickly swept the floor, after stacking the chairs that had been used the night before. Within an hour, the place had been given a good clean down. She grabbed the clean saucepan and made for the door.

'Never would know they'd been,' she said to herself. After putting her coat on, she took a last look around, turned the light off and left. She was driving herself to the hairdressers for her three-monthly perm.

*

There was no chance of Shelley getting Ian up the stairs in the state he was in. She had let him collapse down on the settee. She took his shoes off and threw a blanket over him. From previous experiences she put a bowl on the floor near his head and drummed into him that it was there, and there would be hell to pay in the morning if he was sick on the carpet. No sympathy was displayed for him when she heard him throwing up at least twice during the night.

He was to spend the next four days laid up in bed with what was self-diagnosed as a sickness and diarrhoea virus. He felt a little better after nearly a week, but was rushed into hospital after ten days with kidney and liver failure. He lingered on for nearly a year with dialysis treatments and died when they failed to find a donor.

Sam Crossley now shared a rented house with two other men in Mynydd Du. His two housemates had office jobs and girlfriends in the city, and the two of them were good friends. They spent most of their time in Cardiff, but kept paying their share of the rent on the house, so they had a bolt hole to go to. Or if things went pear shaped with their girlfriends. They didn't really have much to do with Sam. He was too brash for them, and they were very much aware of how he earned his money.

Sam had walked the mile or so home from The Den alone. The house was empty. Apart from feeling very stoned and pretty drunk, he wasn't in bad shape. He rolled himself a fat joint and smoked it with a can of cider before he crashed.

It wasn't until 4.00am, after shitting in his bed, that the poison started to take a hold. He made his way in the dark to the bathroom, knelt down naked at the toilet and began retching his insides out. The mix of the marijuana, alcohol and toxins, combined with the uncontrollable heaving from his stomach proved too much and he passed out. He was found by one of his housemates on Sunday evening. He had choked to death on his own vomit.

Johnny Hill never even made it home. He lived in a converted outbuilding on his parent's farm. He had always been a bitter disappointment to his father, not taking the farm on.

But Johnny hated farming and, as soon as he was old enough to challenge his father, had stopped working there altogether. He had been in the same class as Byron at school and, because he was over six foot, mean looking and as strong as an ox, he was taken into the close circle with open arms. He had been transporting narcotics all over Wales and working the doors for good money ever since.

As he approached the outbuilding, he started to feel nauseous, dizzy and disorientated. He left the path and headed down towards the river. Reaching the edge, he dropped to his knees. Cupping his hands, he scooped up the cold water and splashed his face, and then threw up into the rippling water. The dizziness was overwhelming, so he moved away from the water and sat down, leaning his back against a tree. That's where he passed out.

About four hours later he came around. The pain in his back was excruciating and the dizziness was affecting his vision. Groaning in agony and confusion, he crawled to what he thought was the opening into the field, but he was actually crawling further into the undergrowth. He passed out again.

The following days, his family and friends did a sweep of the riverbank, and found nothing. It was ten days later that his body was found, decomposing in the undergrowth.

Terry Owens only had a small helping of the curry. His mam had fed him shepherds' pie earlier that afternoon, so he wasn't that hungry at the card game. However, the amount he had consumed was enough to concern his loving mother, and she drove him to the hospital on the Friday. The overworked doctor at A&E deduced it was food poisoning and put him on strong dose of antibiotics.

Terry was to suffer with kidney failure for the rest of his life. His weight plummeted to around seven stone, and he never did any kind of work again. Legitimate or not.

Barry Wilkins didn't consume any of the poisoned curry. He had always been a home cooked, traditional meal kind of man, but what he witnessed over the next few days frightened him to the core.

Although he had known Byron for years, he didn't consider himself as a full-time employee of the Lewis crew. Byron used him to do some rent and drug debt collecting, but that was about it. Mostly he worked as a builder, a trade he had learned from his father.

Three weeks later, and with the help, blessing and encouragement of his family, Barry did a disappearing act with his wife and two children in the middle of the night. He was never seen or heard of again.

As for Anthony Rigden, his symptoms went the same way as everybody else, and Sybil absolutely and stubbornly, would not even consider the thought that it was food poisoning. All kinds of viruses and bugs were suggested, but she was adamant, it wasn't her cooking – anyone who even breathed the words 'food poisoning' was given a verbal battering!

She nursed her boy for nearly two weeks, and when the sickness, diarrhoea and dizziness subsided, she was confident that the worse was over. Three days later, after excruciating stomach and back pain, she finally submitted and called the ambulance.

It was difficult for the hospital to diagnose, as it had been so long since consumption. Sybil had been meticulously cleaning up after her son, and encouraging him to eat soup, but they were confident that is was something he had eaten that had destroyed his liver and kidneys. Sybil was mortified. Anthony Rigden died in hospital five days later. Two of those days he was in a coma. His family were at his bedside when the life support was turned off.

Michael Lewis, unlike his big brother Byron, had always been a sickly child. He was four years younger and a lot smaller than his brother. All through their childhood Michael had always been the one to get a cough or to catch a cold.

Byron and Michael's mother had run off with an insurance salesman when Byron was fifteen. It had been a case of good riddance as far as Byron was concerned. She had always been a pain in the arse.

In school, Michael would pick fights and arguments with other kids, and then rely on his big brother to sort them out for him. Byron, of course, relished this because he was a bully. There was nothing he liked better than beating on other kids. Bigger or smaller!

Michael was also not as savvy as Byron, not academically or financially. Byron had a racket going in school, where the weaker kids paid him their dinner money for his protection. He would also sell bottles of cider and cigarettes to kids at the youth club.

Despite this, Byron was very protective of his little brother. Any sleight, insult or injury to his brother was an insult to him and anyone who delivered anything of that nature would be violently dealt with. When Byron had first started working for the Wilton crew he had sub-let some of his fetching and collecting errands to his younger sibling as a way of bringing him into the fold. Byron hated that end of the business anyway. He saw it as below his capabilities. Even back then he had his eyes on bigger things.

It was Saturday morning and Byron was at his childhood home, standing at the end of the bed with his little brother, who was at death's door. Michael's skin had turned grey and clammy and he had been violently ill since Thursday morning. His father hadn't been overly concerned until the Friday morning, when things appeared to be getting worse. He called the doctor out, who said that it was probably a bug and prescribed some medicine to stop the stomach spasms.

Throughout his childhood and adolescence, Michael had suffered numerous kidney infections, so when Michael started mumbling incoherently, his father called the doctor out again. With it being a Saturday, the doctor couldn't get to the house until 10.30am. As soon as he saw Michael he told them to call an ambulance.

The ambulance didn't take long to arrive. Michael was loaded onto a stretcher and whisked off to the local hospital, accompanied by his father. Full lights and sirens.

Byron stood outside the house until the ambulance was out of sight. Absolutely blind with rage he got back into the passenger seat of the waiting BMW. He had made a lot of enquiries since Thursday morning and was convinced he knew what had happened.

'Where the fuck is he, Pete? And how the fuck did he get inside the café? You tell me, Pete.'

Pete had been rocked by all of this. This was really scary stuff. Sonny had announced that he was back, and with more than just a bang! Unless they killed him first, they were marked men.

'Marcus, Sean and Dave have taken a car each and they're out looking for him now. Knocking on doors. If someone is hiding him, we'll fucking get him! But we're low on numbers, Byron.'

Pete noticed that Byron was wide-eyed and twitchy, and was also grinding his teeth. This usually meant he was coked up and liable to go off like a stick of dynamite at any moment.

Byron impatiently searched the inside pockets of his blazer for his fat bag of cocaine.

'I'm going to fucking kill that little bastard. Get everybody you can out there. Call in any favours!'

He dropped the door of the glove compartment to pour a mound of coke for chopping up.

'Don't you think you should ease off that for the time being, By? At least until we're back in control of this fucking lot.'

Byron looked at Pete like a rabid dog ready to pounce. He stared at Pete as if he'd grown another head. 'You fucking what, you cheeky bastard?' he retorted.

'I'm just saying… the best decisions are made with a clear head… not a head full of Charlie.'

In a split-second Byron reached a hand behind Pete's head, smashed his own head toward him, violently butting his best friend straight on the nose.

'DON'T YOU EVER TRY TO LECTURE ME ON ANYTHING EVER AGAIN YOU WANKER. MATES OR NOT, YOU WORK FOR ME. YOU DO AS YOU'RE FUCKING TOLD! NO FUCKING QUESTIONS ASKED. GOT IT?!'

Pete reeled back as best he could. He was holding his nose, which had started bleeding quite badly. 'You fucker,' he said, quite calmly. He wasn't afraid of taking on Byron in a stand-up fight, but didn't want a full-blown ruck in the car.

'I'm watching your back night and day, covering up for you when you fuck up, and this is what you do when I try to help you. Well, bollocks to you then!'

Byron wasn't backing down. He'd never backed down from anything or anyone in his life. To him that was a sign of weakness.

'And bollocks to you too, and get out of my fucking car, you're fucking bleeding all over the place. Get home and change and I'll see you back at the yard about three o'clock. Go on, fuck off.'

Pete didn't need telling twice. He was fuming and wanted to put some distance between him and Byron. He let himself out of the car. Byron got out of the passenger side and walked around the car to get in the drivers' seat.

'Three o'clock!' he shouted after Pete, who had already started to walk home.

Pete shot back a one fingered salute over his shoulder .

Byron laughed as he got in the drivers' seat. He chopped and snorted up the fat line of coke, and then fired up the BMW. He beeped the horn at Pete as he drove past him.

CHAPTER TWENTY-SEVEN
Reason to Kill

Sonny had been kept up-to-date on all the events since Wednesday night via the phone conversations to Arthur, who always made sure Sonny knew of Rhian's progress at the hospital first, before he filled him in on the unfolding drama concerning Byron Lewis.

Arthur, at first, had to search his conscience. He had guessed what Sonny was doing to destroy the Lewis crew, and it did make him uncomfortable. But his daughter could have been killed, and for what? Being under suspicion for knowing where her boyfriend was hiding out! Even if she had told them where to find him, the knowledge that she had played a part in getting him killed would have haunted her for the rest of her life.

In the early hours of Saturday morning Sonny found a safe viewing spot of Pete's flat. Arthur had told him that the driver of the Land Rover, that mowed down his grandmother, was Pete.

He knew that the garage opened for business at 9.00am, but a young apprentice mechanic would normally pull the shutter door up at around 8.00am, so Sonny decided to visit

Pete's flat at 7.45am. Wearing surgical gloves under military gloves, he popped the door open in no time.

He was surprised not to find a hallway or another door behind the fire door, but instead a kitchen. It was small, pokey and sparsely equipped. An old-fashioned cooker and a fridge were the only electrical items. There was a gap next to the sink, where the washing machine should have been. Apart from empty spirit bottles and glasses on the work surfaces, it didn't look as if any cooking had been done for a long time.

Sonny left the kitchen and entered the large living room. The smell of stale booze and cigarettes hung in the air.

A cheap leather three-piece suite took up most of the room. There was a television on a unit in the corner, with a slimline VHS video player underneath. A large, heavy wooden coffee table occupied the middle of the room, with a full ashtray on one corner, and some old magazines on a shelf underneath. The only unusual thing in the room was a massively equipped set of weights and bars in another corner. The only attractive feature being the old farmhouse-style exposed beams on the ceiling.

A tall unit stood against a wall, with a row of drawers making up the bottom half. Sonny had a quick look through all four drawers. Not really knowing what he was looking for, he inevitably found nothing of interest.

He left the living space via a door at the far end of the room. After a quick look in the bathroom, he went into the bedroom. A large, unmade double bed, with a bedside cabinet, was underneath a large window with the thin curtains pulled shut. A large wardrobe containing various clothes and jackets stood to his right. He was just about to leave the room when he spotted a securely padlocked metal cabinet. Beside it was a very large photographer's bag and, after taking a mental picture on how he had found it, Sonny meticulously opened it up to find four cameras. Not expensive ones with varying lenses, but cheap Polaroid cameras. Trying to come up with a logical reason for the find, Sonny sat and puzzled this for a few seconds. He checked his watch: 10.15am.

Then, he heard the heavy footsteps coming up the fire escape. Sonny had thought that it was unlikely that he would see Pete or Byron today, but now it looked like a distinct possibility.

He quickly flicked open his bag and took out a face flannel, and small plastic bottle of ether, of which, he squirted a generous amount onto the flannel. Holding the flannel as far away from his face as he could, he took his ambush position behind the bedroom door.

Pete was more than a little pissed off as he arrived at the steps to his flat. He had received some strange looks as he walked home, even though he had tried his best to stop his nose bleeding. He couldn't breathe through it, so he guessed it was broken. This wouldn't have been the first time.

He entered the kitchen and went straight through into the lounge, shrugging his jacket off and throwing it onto the settee. Deciding that he needed a shower, he emptied his trouser pockets of his wallet and keys, and dropped them onto the coffee table. Gingerly touching his nose and cussing at the pain, he headed for the bedroom to fetch some clean clothes.

With everything that had happened recently Pete should have been more on guard, but he walked straight into a trap.

Sonny latched onto Pete's back. He wrapped an arm around

his chest, and clamped the ether soaked flannel tightly over his mouth. He wrapped both legs around Sawyer's upper waist, pinning his arms to his side. With forward momentum they fell heavily forward onto the bedroom floor.

Pete was, at first, completely shocked by the attack, but within seconds, panic and self-preservation took over. He kicked and bucked like a rodeo bull, in an attempt to free his arms. The pain of the hand clamped around his damaged nose was overpowering him, and he took in huge gulps of the ether fumes. To his credit, he lasted a good minute until he was eventually overcome, and then passed out.

Sonny waited another thirty seconds after Pete's body went limp before he relaxed his grip. Without pausing for breath, he reached into his bag for the heavy-duty cable ties and gaffer tape. He had Pete blindfolded, gagged, hog-tied securely, and lying on his stomach in no time at all. He estimated that it would be between thirty and forty-five minutes until the big man would start to come round.

Finally pausing for breath, he left the bedroom and went into the lounge. He immediately saw Pete's keys on the coffee table. He found the key to the metal cabinet and went back into the bedroom and unlocked it. The top drawer held two more Polaroid cameras, some unused boxes and new Polaroid film. Sonny started to feel slightly uncomfortable at Pete's obsession with instant and cheap photography, especially when he looked into the second and third drawers of the cabinet.

What he found made him sick to the pit of his stomach. There were hundreds of Polaroid pictures of young girls – children. In various stages of undress. Some of them looked as young as seven or eight years old. The oldest looked no more than thirteen, and a lot of them were in school uniform.

Most of the photos showed Pete committing various sex acts on these children, or having sex acts being performed on him, with him grinning at the camera. Bottles of beer and spirits were visible in nearly all the photos. Some of the children were laughing or smiling at the camera, obviously having been intoxicated with alcohol and recreational drugs. But it was obvious that in a lot of the horrifying cheap photos, they looked nervous and scared at what they were being bullied and coerced into doing.

Sonny stopped looking at the disgusting, sordid and depraved images. He wanted to kick Pete to death where he lay. In a blind, determined rage he dragged the unconscious pervert by the shoulders out of the bedroom, through the hallway and into the lounge. Sawyer started to moan as he was dumped in the middle of the room, so Sonny gave him another few breaths of the ether to put him back to sleep. He needed a few minutes to set up what he had planned for the disgusting paedophile.

It was over an hour until Pete came to. The overpowering scent from a bottle of smelling salt wafting under his broken nose somehow managing to get through, and snap him awake. His head was thumping with pain. He had a chemical taste in his mouth, and for a few moments he had no idea where he was.

Soon he realised that he was blindfolded, and after attempting to cry out, also realised that he had been gagged. For a few seconds he purposely didn't move as he weighed up his predicament. It felt almost as if he was suspended. He could feel solid ground beneath his feet, so instinctively tried to stand up.

Sonny started to struggle with the dead weight of the larger man, and swiftly collected the slack from the sheet wrapped around Pete's neck. This makeshift noose was threaded over a beam in the centre of the room. It was then anchored securely to the weights in the corner.

Pete realised the grave position he was in as soon as Sonny undid the blindfold. Looking around in panic he realised that he was standing near the edge of the coffee table. There was a noose around his neck.

Scattered around him were the photographs from the cabinet in the bedroom. Pete instinctively felt the presence of Sonny behind him, and carefully turned to be face-to-face with his young tormentor. He nodded his acknowledgement of defeat to the young man.

'Were you the driver of the Land Rover that killed my grandmother?' Sonny asked calmly.

Pete frowned at first, and then nodded slowly.

'Did you play any part in the murder of my grandfathers two best friends?'

Again, Pete nodded slowly.

'I know you weren't on the mountain when Byron Lewis shot my grandfather because I was there, hiding under the ring apron. But I do know where *you* dumped his body.'

Pete's eyes widened at this revelation.

'*You* took everything away. *You* made me go into hiding. *You* made me come back. *You* made me kill you! And now…'

Sonny moved closer to the coffee table.

'You *were* going to die by my hands today Pete Sawyer, but after finding this.' He waved a handful of the disgusting images in front of his face. 'I'm going to give you the chance to do it yourself. Jump before you're pushed so to speak. Monsters like you need to be caught and killed, don't they?'

Pete gulped.

'Then I'm going after Byron Lewis, and he will pay.'

Pete made a motion with his head, almost like he wanted to say something.

Sonny reached up and removed the soft tea cloth he had used as a gag. He didn't want to leave any tape or glue marks from gaffer tape. He also offered Pete a large swig from a half bottle of scotch that he had found in the kitchen, which he gulped down greedily. This would mask the smell of the ether. Sonny planned to splash it around his bloodied shirt later. Now that Sawyer had willingly gulped it down had saved him the bother.

'He's gone stark… raving… fucking… mad. You fucking killed his brother! So you'd better be on top of your game, boy,' Pete warned him.

'I am, believe me. Anything else?' Sonny queried. 'There's a gun, a revolver. He keeps it in the top drawer of his desk at the scrapyard. He likes to wave it round if he's threatening or intimidating someone, but he most definitely plans to use it to finish you if he gets the chance. It's the same one he used to kill your grandfather and his friends. The mad bastard thinks it would be brilliant if he gets to shoot you with it too.'

Pete then looked at Sonny with resignation. He screwed his eyes and mouth tight shut and stepped off the coffee table. The noose snapped tight around his neck as he dropped the few inches needed.

Sonny swiftly pulled the table away from Pete's reach, and then stood away. He felt no pity or remorse, just that rightful justice had been served.

Pete's body convulsed violently, his tethered feet kicked out in protest, but it only took about twenty seconds until he lost consciousness, and the convulsions were reduced to twitches.

Sonny got to work as soon as Pete's body had stopped moving. After checking he was very much dead, he cut off the cable ties binding his arms and feet, purposely positioning the dead man's arms at his side. The cable ties had been deliberately tightened over the shirt and trousers so they did not leave any marks. The coffee table was pushed back into its original position. Pete Sawyer killed himself!

Sonny quickly gathered everything up he had used. He was still wearing surgical gloves underneath his military gloves. The ether soaked flannel was sealed into a freezer bag as soon as it was no longer to be used, to reduce the smell.

Once he was satisfied that all traces of him being there were in his kit bag, he did the role play that Patch had taught him…

He was Pete and had just entered the flat in a distressed state, with the intention of hanging himself. He threw his jacket on the settee, and went to the cabinet to get the photos, scattering them all around him.

After knocking back some whisky, he went back into the bedroom and pulled the sheet from the bed. He tore it up and made a strong noose. He secured one end to the gym weights and, after poking a big enough hole in the ceiling, looped the noose over the beam. Standing on the coffee table with the noose around his neck, he killed himself. He could no longer live with the man he'd become!

After one final sweep of the flat, Sonny left through the back entrance. It was 1.15pm. Opening the rear exit door a few inches, he risked a quick look down and around. It had been raining so the street behind the garage was quiet. He could hear the sound of air tools being used in the garage out front, so he made his way down the stairs as quickly and as quietly as he could. Once down on street level, he zipped his coat up to his chin and pulled the hood over his head. Then, as calmly as he could, he stepped out onto the pavement.

He had to get to the cemetery. A food parcel was waiting for him at the graveside of Arthur's mother! Under the pretext of paying his respects, Arthur had cunningly concealed some sandwiches, a packet of biscuits, and some fruit into a big bunch of flowers!

Sonny replaced the flowers, as neatly as he could, back on the grave of Elsie Hughes. He leapt the wall at the rear of the cemetery into an adjacent field, and headed back to the hideout. After everything this morning, he was totally exhausted. He needed food and rest, and to gather his thoughts. On his way back, he made the detour to the phone box and called Arthur to tell him he had retrieved the food and thanked him.

When Sonny told Arthur that Pete was dead he was at first shocked by news. After all, this Sonny was supposed to be marrying his daughter! Once Sonny explained about the cameras and hundreds of sordid Polaroid's he had discovered, Arthur was adamant that he would have strung up the perverted bastard himself had he been in the room. Also, the fact that Pete had admitted and not contradicted or denied his involvement in the murders of Sonny's family was enough to convince him that justice, and not wanton murder, had been meted out.

It was late afternoon and it was raining steadily by the time Sonny reached his place of safety. After covering the hideout for better water proofing, he retrieved his large rucksack and made his way to the spring, where he washed and changed his clothes. Back at the hideout, he ate.

Now, he had to decide whether to stand back for a while and let the repercussions of Pete's death play out. Or to keep up the momentum and strike again. He decided on the former. He suspected that Byron wouldn't buy into the suicide pervert scenario, and be very much on high alert at least for the first twenty-four hours.

He correctly reasoned that Byron would play along, and order everyone in his circle to play along with the authorities. His best friend snapped and committed suicide because he couldn't control his perversion for little girls. That would die down quicker than if murder was suspected and allow Byron to continue trying to hunt Sonny down and flush him out.

Sonny needed to rest. He climbed into his warm sleeping bag and lay on his back thinking of his grandparents. Would they have approved of what he was doing? He was sure his grandfather would have. He had always hated Byron and his plans. His mind went back to the morning on the mountain when he witnessed the first confrontation between Alf and Byron and he had put that big gorilla on his back.

He thought of his lovely Rhian. As he slowly drifted into sleep, he dared himself to dream of a life with the only girl he would ever love. A life when this was all over. There was still so much to overcome, and so much that could go wrong.

CHAPTER TWENTY-EIGHT
Breaking the News

Byron spent Saturday night in a room that he kept at *The Night Owl*. It was a room that he used if he was out late on business and didn't want to disturb his girlfriend, Lizzie.

As powerful as he thought he was, he had to admit that he was a little unnerved at how close Sonny Wilton was getting. For safety he was going to move around; not stay in one place for long. He even gave one doorman a wedge to stay awake all night and patrol all the entry points of the club.

To make matters worse, Byron had received a call late Saturday evening, telling him that his little brother had slipped into a coma and it didn't look good. He couldn't decide if he was grieving or raging when he requested that Marcus and Sean join him at the club with a bag full of cocaine and copious amounts of booze. And where was Pete? The little bastard hadn't shown up at three o'clock as ordered. Byron concluded that his right-hand man was still sulking. *Bollocks to him*, he thought. *They all need reminding once in a while about who calls the shots, even Pete.*

Byron woke in the morning feeling quite sick and with a thumping hangover. After getting dressed, he freshened himself up in the night club washroom. Remembering what had happened at *The Den* he took no chances and bought himself a sandwich and a bottle of orange juice from a delicatessen, and ate his breakfast in the BMW.

When he'd finished, he tapped out a small mound of cocaine onto his wallet and snorted it up with a rolled-up note. He needed to sharpen himself up he told himself. Before setting off he called Pete's flat again, to see if he had stopped moping. A voice he didn't recognise answered.

'Hullo, who is this?' It was an official sounding voice.

Byron hung up immediately.

Puzzled? Worried? He wasn't sure how he felt as he got back in the car and headed back towards Mynydd Du.

It was 11.00am when he arrived at the scrapyard. No real work was done in the yard on a Sunday, but Saville still opened the gates and did a bit of cleaning up in the morning. DC Sharpe was waiting for Byron in an unmarked police vehicle. Byron had a deep feeling of dread as he got out of the car. He didn't speak to the detective. He thought if he ignored him, the problem would go away.

'Can I have a word?' asked DC Sharpe. 'OK,' replied Byron.

Saville looked solemnly at the two of them as they went up the steps to the office.

Byron unlocked the office door and they went inside. He went straight to the chair behind the desk and dropped himself on it. The detective remained standing.

'Well?' Byron asked, raising two open hands.

'Pete Sawyer was found dead in the living room of his home address this morning by a Miss Melanie Grahams. She has identified herself as his on-off girlfriend. She let herself into the flat at 9.00am with her own key.'

Byron's face started to twitch with the shock. This news appeared to hit him hard. He stood up from the chair and ran a hand through his hair.

'Old Mrs Grahams will have a lot of leftovers for bubble and squeak tomorrow then, won't she?' he commented, with his trademark morbid humour. In truth, he was rocked to the core.

DC Sharpe continued, 'He had apparently killed himself. The cause of death was hanging between midday and five yesterday afternoon, although he did appear to have sustained a blow to the nose.'

'I did that!' Byron immediately confessed.

'We had a bit of a fallout yesterday. He was getting out of line, so I nutted him. He went home in a strop to change his shirt. I was supposed to meet him at three, but he didn't show!' Byron sat back in the chair totally dumbfounded. 'He fucking hanged himself because of that?'

The detective let out a deep sigh before he carried on. He reached into his coat pocket and pulled out three of the worst photos from the scene, and dropped them on the desk. 'I don't think so. It might have pushed him over the edge, but I think it was probably this. There was approximately three hundred of these photos scattered around the body.'

Byron picked up the photos. He looked in pain as he took in the depraved scene of each one. He knew Pete had a penchant for the younger girls. But this? What the fuck?! *These are children the dirty sick bastard*, he thought. 'So, what are we saying here, Sharpey, he couldn't live with himself because I gave him a smack yesterday?

He took out all these filthy stinking pictures, tossed them in the air and hung his fucking self, yeah?' Even Byron couldn't stand looking at the photos any longer and he threw them back on the desk. The detective put them back into his pocket.

'That's how it looks, Byron. When Miss Grahams found him, with all those photographs around his body, she called the police. She said she felt duty bound for the sake of those children. Pete's body has been taken to the mortuary, and now you've cleared up the nose injury line of enquiry there probably won't be a post mortem. I'm guessing here, but I think the family will want to put this all behind them as quickly and quietly as possible.' Byron looked defiantly at DC Sharpe. He wanted to come back at him with something, but knew that it made sense to get this out of the way as soon as possible. It didn't look good that his best friend was a kiddy fiddler. 'OK, the carrier of all good news, you can fucking go.' The detective opened the door of the office to leave, then turned back to Byron.

'Is there any progress on Sonny Wilton? It seems that some at the nick are questioning the food poisoning story. Some reckon it was done on purpose. If the powers-that-be decide to take that line of enquiry, it'll be out of my hands.'

Byron stared at Pete's favourite chair and for a second did not answer. He turned to look at Sharpe. 'No there fucking isn't. Don't worry, when I find him you'll be one of the first to know. If you know what I mean.'

The corrupt police officer left the office, and Byron watched as he got back in his car and drove out of the scrapyard.

Just thinking about Sonny Wilton set Byron's coke muddled brain into meltdown. Drumming his fingers on the desk, he began wrestling with his memories of the last few days.

Nobody knew Pete as well he did! They knew each other inside out. True, Byron didn't know about his perversion for little girls, but that was the kind of thing you kept hidden from *everyone*.

Pete hadn't seemed stressed or depressed about anything. Over half the crew had been poisoned, but Pete had handled it as he did everything. 'See what happens,' was his favourite mantra every time the shit hit the fan. Pete hang himself?! Byron just couldn't believe it. Sent over the edge because of a little ruck? Really? They had knocked the hell out of each other over the years, so why now?

Could Sonny Wilton have murdered Pete and been clever enough to make it look like suicide? The more he thought about it, the more he was convinced that this was so. It was convenient for everyone to let Pete's passing go down as a suicide, but when he finally did get that little bastard under his control, he would torture him mercilessly for what he did to his best mate. Never mind what kind of sick pervert he was.

The phone rang in the office. All calls concerning the scrapyard went to a separate number in the shed outside, so all calls to the office were personal – or other business!

It was the hospital. His brother was fading fast. Byron quickly unlocked the top drawer of the desk and took out the Webley revolver that was carefully wrapped in a lightly oiled cleaning rag. He unwrapped the gun and broke open the barrel, shaking out all six bullets. He inspected each loading chamber. After a quick polish, he loaded the bullets back up. He then relocated the chamber and locked the barrel. He carefully wrapped the gun back up in the cloth and replaced it in the drawer.

After locking up he left for the same hospital that Rhian was currently recovering in. The evil in him toyed with dropping by the ward with some flowers to say hello, but commonsense prevailed. *Best stay clear there*, he thought. *Don't want to bring any unwanted attention.*

Byron couldn't understand why he felt more sorrow about the death of his best friend, than the impending death of his own flesh and blood. *Oh well, we are who we are*, he thought.

He couldn't stay at his brother's bedside for more than an hour. The hissing sound of the respirator and beeping of other machines was driving him insane. Michael's kidneys had never functioned properly all his life and the trauma of the poison toxins, or whatever it was, had rendered them inactive. He needed a donor immediately, but he probably wouldn't survive that kind of major surgery if one was found. There was also his dodgy liver. He had been in a coma since Saturday evening and would not last the night.

Byron gave his little brother a token kiss on the forehead and left. His father was going to stay with Michael until the end. His mother was nowhere to be found.

Seeing as he was already in Cardiff, before he left the hospital, Byron made a call to John Jones, the manager at *The Night Owl*. He told him that he would be staying there again tonight. The club was obviously closed on a Sunday night, but he told John to have the bar open privately, as he would be having a few quiet drinks with some close friends. He'd give the back-entry door a bang around nine.

Byron then called Marcus Evans and told him to get hold of Sean Ramsey and Dave Wood. If they could round up a few others, especially a few women, all the better. They were going to get a load of drink down them tonight. And send Michael and Pete on their way. A private wake if you like.

Before he hung up the phone on Marcus, he was told that the body of Sam Crossley had been found by the side of the toilet at his house. He had choked to death on his own sick. Byron slammed the phone back on the receiver and kicked the wall.

CHAPTER TWENTY-NINE
Cat and Mouse

Sonny rigorously thought through his next plan during Sunday as he rested at the hideout. It certainly was a good plan, but after he phoned Patch and ran him through it, he wasn't so sure. There were a lot of things that could go wrong. He told his mentor that since Wednesday, Byron had been moving around, and was never in one place for very long. So, relying on him being in one place long enough to launch an ambush was going to be near to impossible.

Patch wasn't confident that Sonny's plan was the best way to draw him out. In fact, it looked quite the opposite. Then again, maybe it was genius plan after all, as he'd planned his getaway meticulously.

Sonny made a few astute phone calls in an attempt to find Byron. He eventually tracked down the landlord of the *Vauxhall* pub.

'He'll go absolutely ape shit if you don't pass on this message, so it's up to you,' threatened Sonny.

'All right, all right, don't get shirty!' replied the landlord, as he shouted over the song coming from the jukebox. It was playing *I Will Always Love You* by Whitney Houston.

'They're having a so-called wake for Michael Lewis and Pete Sawyer at *The Night Owl* in town. Now, you didn't get the number from me, OK.'

Apart from Sean and Dave, Marcus had managed to get another thirteen others to join them for what was really a booze and drugs session disguised as a wake. Five of them were barmaids and waitresses at *The Night Owl*, and the other club *Options*. The banter was pretty good and there was plenty of alcohol being put away, plus a fair few lines being snorted. John Jones had put on the *1992 Greatest Hits* CD from the DJ booth.

A lot of Byron's guests gave the impression that they were there under duress. It was Sunday night after all, and most of them had jobs to get up for in the morning, even if some of them did work for Byron. Byron started to get the hump at this lack of enthusiasm, and by midnight he was deep into a morose and nasty mood. No amount of alcohol or drugs was going to drag him out of it!

Out of earshot, the phone rang behind the bar. John approached Byron, who was sitting there nursing a large whisky.

'There someone on the phone, boss,' said John. 'He says it's urgent.'

Byron immediately assumed it was his father calling from the hospital to tell him that his brother had passed, as he was the only one that had a direct contact number for him. Everyone else knew better than to give out his personal contact information.

He drained his glass and winced as the cheap scotch hit the back of his throat. Blowing out his cheeks with a huge breath, he went to the end of the bar where the phone receiver had been left and put it to his ear.

'Hullo.' He prepared himself for the news from his father.

'Hello, Mr Lewis.' The reply was calm, measured. 'Is this the hospital?' asked Byron, not recognising the voice on the other end. Thinking his father might have been too upset to make the call.

'I just wanted to let you know how sorry I was for your recent… losses.' It sounded like the man was deliberately pausing before the last word.

'Wilton!' Byron snapped sharply, although he had never actually heard Sonny Wilton speak before, ever.

'Where have you been for so long, Wilton?' Byron asked, trying to sound as calm as possible, even though he had been knocked sideways by the call. This, he had not been expecting.

He signalled for John to go and kill the music with a cut throat gesture. John complied and went and sat with the others. Conversations were reduced to whispers.

'Dealing with my own losses, Mr Lewis, you know how it is. Can I call you, Byron?' Sonny asked.

'You can call me what you like for now, Wilton.' 'How about murderer? Does that sound comfortable enough for you?'

'Murderer! Well, you'd know about that if the last couple of days are anything to go by,' Byron retorted.

'I have no idea what you're trying to imply.' Sonny's voice remained calm.

'How did you do it, Wilton? How the fuck did you manage to do it, and not one of my lads notice a fucking thing?' Byron started to lose his composure.

'I have the right to remain silent and that's what I'm going to do if that's OK with you,' said Sonny.

'I think you're a sneaky cowardly bastard if that's OK with you,' replied Byron.

'I was there, Mr Lewis… on the mountain… when you murdered my grandfather. So, I can confidently call you a murderer.'

'Bollocks, if you were there you'd be dead and buried where he is.' Byron's mind flew back to the gym on the mountain. 'Alf was on his own. We had a little chat about the terrible car accident with your grandmother, and he gave me the old lecture and… well the rest is history. The ring was burnt down. You weren't there. You're talking shit, Wilton.'

'I was under the ring apron when you shot him. I sat there listening to him die and watched his blood drip through the canvas. I crawled out of the back of the ring into the bushes and watched the ring go up in flames. Morganstown pit shaft A. I was there.'

Byron digested that piece of news and then silently cursed to himself. He could have had it all sewn up in the mountain gym that day.

'Well, you're one lucky, sneaky, cowardly, bastard, ain't you, Wilton? For the time being, at least.'

'The bastard who killed my grandmother has been dealt with though, hasn't he? I find that a comfort.'

'You fucking killed him, didn't you, Wilton?'

'No, I didn't. I was there, but he killed himself. Just after he realised he was going to get found out.' Sonny paused. 'As for the man watching the hospital… he took one for the team… that is until the real woman beater gets caught up with!'

There was a silence as Byron gritted his teeth, doing his best to swallow his temper.

'I'm going to find you, Wilton, and I'm gonna kill you. Me! That's a promise. You are the last grape. I need to crush you, so I can enjoy the wine. I like that, do you like that?'

'Yeah, I like that Byron, because I'll be the poison grape in the wine.'

Byron slammed a huge fist onto the bar and started spitting his words. 'You, dirty, sneaky, coward. Come out into the open you yellow bastard. Fucking hiding in the shadows, waiting for a chance to shoot me in the back. Come and face me like a man you fucking snake!' The whispering crowd in the club fell to a stunned silence as Byron lost control, but Sonny seemed totally calm. *Was this what he wanted*? thought Byron. *To goad him.*

'What are you saying, Byron? You want to fight me man to man?'

'Fucking right, I'll fight you man to man. I'll batter you to death, you snake, and then I'll rip your fucking arms and legs off. I'll have you buried in shoe boxes all round the country, you little shit.'

'I'll fight you fair and square, Byron. What do you suggest?'

'Any fucking time, any fucking where!' Byron snapped back. A plan was scratching around his head. This could all work in his favour.

Sonny continued, 'There used to be a transportable ring all packed up at the boxing club. I'm sure you can get the manpower to get it up to the old gym on the mountain and set it up.'

Byron cheered sarcastically down the receiver.

'Oh yeah! Just like the old days, is it? King of the coal stuff. Winner takes the reins. I love it. Bring it on.'

'Problem is, I don't trust you as far as I can throw you, Byron, and you're a big strong man, so I won't be able to throw you far.'

Byron sounded almost insulted. 'I won't need any fun and games to take you out, Wilton! I can't promise I'm gonna fight to strict Queensbury rules, but I can do the job by myself. Don't you fucking worry. I'll also have as many people from around town as I can muster to witness the great spectacle. How about that?'

'OK, how about Tuesday, midday?'

'No fucking problem, see you there, Wilton. Don't coward out on me, will you?'

'Can't wait, Byron, can't wait.'

Byron hung up and walked over to the now silent group of drinkers and ordered everyone out, except Marcus, Sean and Dave. The party was over. There was skullduggery to be discussed. They would be there until 3.00am.

Sonny hung up and left the phone box. It was just outside the scrapyard. After placating Saville's guard dog, who recognised Sonny straight away from better times, he forced the padlock open and entered the scrapyard. After ruffling the big dog's ears, he headed for the office, with the dog skipping playfully alongside him. This shouldn't take too long.

In the dark hours of Monday morning, Sonny destroyed the hideout that been his shelter for the last week. He packed everything into the rucksack and made the long journey across the fields and up the far side of the mountain. As he arrived he made sure that no one was around, and then looked over at the weight set that was still there, beside the thick posts where the heavy bag used to hang. He also noticed the old log, where he used to sit so many times with his grandfather, and where he frantically dug up the plastic container that fateful day. He had to tear himself away and cautiously made his way down the path on the other side. The gate to the now boarded up family home had become overgrown with weeds and ivy, so he had to go through the hedge and up to the side of the house. The padlock on the cellar door had rusted, so he had no choice but to risk making the noise, and smash it off. Going down the familiar five steps he put his head torch on, and made his way up the stairs on the far side. Easily picking the lock on the door, he entered into the hallway of his home.

As he entered the large kitchen a feeling of sadness immersed him. The windows were boarded up and it was dark, but he could tell that nothing had been touched. There was a layer of dust over everything and a damp odour hung in the air. Everything was the same. The kitchen furniture. The dishes. The tinned food still in the pantry. There was even a mouldy half loaf in the bread bin. Unwashed dishes in the sink. A pile of unopened mail sat underneath the front door.

He wandered from room to room; memories flooding back as he did so. Once all this was over he would tear down the boards and make this a Wilton home again!

He snapped himself out of his reverie and double-checked every room to make sure that no one had been in the house at all these last six months. Satisfied that he was probably safe here until midday tomorrow he decided to stick to the kitchen.

From there he had three possible routes of escape. The back door, the front door, or into the hallway and down into the cellar. While he still had the protection of the dark, he went outside and cut a small hole from a corner of the boarding, so he could see the back gate and the mountain path.

Having had very little to eat and not much sleep during the previous night, he quickly scoffed down the food that he had brought with him, as well as a cold tin of beans from the pantry. He rolled out the camping mattress and sleeping bag in the corner of the kitchen and, maybe because of the comfort of being in his own house, for a few hours, at least, he slept quite soundly.

He snapped awake to the sound of voices. His watch told him it just after 11.00am and, arming himself with the commando knife and cosh, he leapt out of the sleeping bag. He stood concrete still so he could determine where, and how close, the voices were. There were about four to six men, Sonny guessed, and they were coming up the mountain path. Looking through the hole he had made earlier, he saw six men carrying three long and heavy looking boxes. Over the next hour they made two more trips down and back up the path. Sonny made an educated guess that the six men were putting up the boxing ring.

It was nearly 5.00pm and getting quite dark when the six men made their way back down the mountain. Sonny's hands and feet were numb with cold, but he left it another thirty minutes, so the night sky and the darkness of the mountain would be his allies as he left the house through the cellar door, and up to the mountain gym. He didn't want to use a torch in case the beam was spotted from further down, so he squatted down behind the garden hedge to allow his eyes to accustom themselves as best they could to the dark.

When he reached the mountain top, he found it surreal to see the boxing ring back exactly in the place where the old one had stood. He found himself again thinking about the day he had hidden underneath the apron, listening to his grandfather being shot. Once again he could feel the sadness rising in his chest, but this time it was mixed with anger and rage. Tomorrow, this was all going to be over. Looking up into the black sky, he silently asked for the gods of justice to ride with him. His grandparents had never drummed religion into him, but he wouldn't turn his back on some kind of divine help.

Sonny decided to call Arthur as he didn't know if he'd get another chance. Maybe ever! Not taking any chances of using a phone box in the town, he made his way back through the fields to the one he had been using all week. Arthur answered at the first ring.

'Hello, Arthur Hughes.' 'Evening, Arthur. How's Rhian?'

'They let her come home today, Sonny. We've set the small bed up in the downstairs front room for her.'

Sonny couldn't understand why Arthur wasn't sounding more upbeat. Then realised what was coming. 'We've all been 'summoned' up to the old mountain gym tomorrow at midday. Have you lost your senses, son?'

Sonny tried his best to sound as if he knew exactly what he was doing. 'It's the only way to end this sooner rather than later, Arthur.'

'Surely you don't think he's going to play this straight? There's bound to be a trap and he's going to kill you. Byron has also requested that Alf's old business associates be up there to *convince* them to team up with him and his business. So, he's pretty confident that he's going to come out on top tomorrow.'

'Then I'd better make sure that what I have planned comes off, and he doesn't come out on top.'

'It's Byron Lewis, the psychopath, Sonny. There must be another way. Challenging him to the old fair fight on the mountain, it's crazy!'

'I know, but I've put things in place. Set some things up, that will hopefully work in my favour,' he tried to reassure him.

'Things in place? Set things up?' Arthur sounded panicked. 'If you get the chance you are going to have to kill him! There, in the ring, on top of the mountain. Son, I do fancy your chances there believe me, but what happens if you do beat him fair and square in a fist fight. He's not going to shake your hand and walk away with his tail between his legs.' He paused to allow his words to sink in. 'He'll have you from behind in the middle of the night and kill you; like he nearly did with Rhian.'

There were a few seconds of silence before Sonny spoke.

'It's too late, Arthur, everything is in place. If I don't show tomorrow he'll win anyway. They'll all believe that he's the new king as the only man to challenge him was too much of a coward to turn up. Remember this, I challenged him. What would I do? Where would I go? What life could I possibly offer Rhian? Looking over our shoulders everywhere we went.'

There was another silence, Sonny could hear Arthur sighing heavily.

'I have to do this. I need to do this. Win or lose. Kill or be killed.'

Arthur sounded defeated. 'I'll be there with you, Son. If I can do anything I will.'

'No, please. Don't do anything that may get you hurt. You know what he is capable of.'

'OK,' said Arthur, but he didn't sound convincing in his compliance. 'I'll carry the phone through to Rhian for you to talk.'

After a few seconds Sonny could hear a door shut and, for what felt like had been forever, he heard his lovely girlfriend's voice.

'Hello, my lovely man.'

'Hello, sweetie. How you doing?'

'Better by the day. Better for hearing your voice.' 'You know, don't you?'

'Yes, I know, and yes, I don't want you to go there. But I know you will. I know you have to do this. My parents want to give us their life savings for us to disappear somewhere. I refused, of course, and I've told them that whatever happens, Sonny Wilton will have done what he had to do.'

'Thank you, sweetie.'

'Get it done, Sonny. Get it done and tear him down.

Then come back to us. Back to me.' 'I will. I promise.'

'And you can replace this hairband on my finger with something else.' She said jokingly.

'We'll see. We'll see. Bye, sweetie.' He smiled genuinely, for what felt the first time in ages, then hung up the phone.

It was coming up to 10.00pm by the time Sonny got back to the house. He washed, changed and ate. Whether he was going to get any sleep tonight, he wasn't sure. But he had to try. Big day tomorrow!

CHAPTER THIRTY
Treachery and Cunning

Sonny spent most of the night working out a plan of escape if the need to run was to arise. Fight another day and all that, he thought. Apart from run like hell, and try to get himself hidden in the countryside, nothing else looked feasible. Not to overlook the fact that he may be seriously injured if things went totally awry. To be honest, he really only had plan A. Plan B would have to be made up on the spot.

He found it difficult to sleep any longer, so he got up, washed and put on his light weight grey track suit. It was 7.00am. He managed to eat some dried fruit. Anything else would have been impossible. He did some light exercises for an hour to get his body flexible and supple, and shadow boxed around the kitchen to keep warm.

Just after 8.00am he heard voices on the path and saw four of the men from yesterday make their way past the gate and up to the gym. He guessed that they were there to check everything was in order. He had noticed that one of the ropes looked a bit slack, but thought better of tightening it himself.

The first witnesses to the proposed spectacle started to go past in ones and twos at around 11.00am. Sonny's stomach was doing somersaults by now as midday was approaching. He recognised some of the other shopkeepers from around the area, and some of his grandfathers' old business associates from Mynydd du and the city. There were quite a few that he didn't recognise, both young and old. Some of the older men pointed to the house as they went past. Arthur Hughes went past at 11.45am. He didn't look at the house, even though he knew Sonny was in there. Altogether he had roughly counted about forty people, all men.

At 12.00am precisely Sonny left the house, his house, out of the back door. He didn't have to hide anymore. It was time for him to come out into the open and be recognised. He walked at a steady pace up the garden path and pulled the garden gate away from the clinging weeds, and started up the mountain path to the gym.

The nerves and panic that had been gnawing away at him all morning had suddenly disappeared. He felt calm, focused, ready!

He saw the three men before they saw him, but when he had been spotted they descended on him like wolves. It was exactly as he thought would happen, and it was down to him to sustain as little damage to his body as he could. Because he couldn't fight back! If he did they would just carry on until he was spent, and very injured. He rolled with some of the punches and kicks, then cried and groaned as loud as he could to feign serious injury and pleaded and begged for them to stop. A technique taught to captured Special Forces soldiers to try and sound beaten and broken, and hopefully bring an end to the assault.

Sonny did all he could to protect his ribs and head, but

trying not to show the three aggressors that he was doing that. He could do nothing about a serious punch to his right eye that was definitely going to puff up.

After he thought he had taken enough to convince them, he let his body go limp, as if he had passed out or lost consciousness.

What happened next had crossed his mind, but he had convinced himself that it wouldn't happen. Not even Byron Lewis would be that much of a coward. His wrists were held in front of him, and a thick cable tie was pulled tight around them.

He was hauled to his feet and half marched and half dragged to the boxing ring and thrown in under the bottom rope. Sonny could hear some disapproving whispers, but mostly there was an uncomfortable silence. He decided he had better stay lying on the canvas for now. Buy some time.

Byron came through the crowd wearing a smart two piece suit and climbed into the ring from the opposite side of where they had pushed Sonny. He started humming the *Rocky* theme tune and doing some shadow boxing.

By the way he was dressed it was obvious to everyone there, he had not come for a fair and square boxing fight.

He took off his jacket and hung it on a corner post, then unbuttoned and folded up the cuffs of his shirt. He then walked over to Sonny, still lying on the canvas. He stooped down to take a look and make sure that the younger man was very much incapacitated. He then stood back up and kicked him in the midriff with a shiny brogue shoe. Sonny, in preparation for something underhanded, absorbed most of the damage from the blow with his folded forearms. It winded him badly and he struggled to get settled air back through his lungs. He pushed himself up to a sitting position and leaned against the ropes. His mind was now racing.

Byron started to walk and loudly address all the men present, on all four sides of the ring. 'I've been running this show for quite a while now, but some of you have failed to come forward and embrace your new management. So, I have decided to ask you all here to witness, finally, the leaving of the very last remnant of the old management.' He pointed to Sonny. 'Now, after today, I expect you all…' He did a sweeping gesture around the whole crowd. '…to come on board the Byron Lewis bus. Those who already have, I thank you. Those that will from now on, I welcome you. Those of you that choose not to, well, if you are not with me then you are against me. You are my enemy. I must fight you.'

'I have always liked the old communist saying that "to make sure you have eliminated your enemy. You must also destroy the roots." So, I will fight your mothers and fathers, brothers and sisters and your sons and daughters, to ensure that I have indeed snuffed out my enemies. I'm not going to kill them! Just make their lives hell, and they will be in no doubt, because I will, of course, inform them, that the misery being dished out to them is because of you, and your unwillingness to board my bus and pay your fucking way.'

He walked slowly back to where Sonny was now sitting. 'By way of letting everyone know that I am the real deal and I am deadly serious.' He looked deep into Sonny's eyes, one of which was bruising and closing already. 'I am going to make an extreme example.'

He leaned forward and spoke quietly into Sonny's ear. 'You didn't really think I was going to fight you in this ring did you, Wilton? I saw what you did to fat Sid remember, and was told in detail what you did to Jay Fowler. I ain't fucking stupid. But you, you're naive as fuck. Just like your poor old gramps. This is quite something really. I get to kill you both, in exactly the same place, except you'll get a sea burial, just like Alf's old buddies.'

Byron smiled and walked back to where he had hung his coat and pulled the Webley revolver from the inside pocket. He had picked it up from the scrapyard that morning. It was in exactly the same place as he had left it Sunday evening after he had checked it. He unwrapped the gun from the soft oiled cloth and put it straight in his jacket.

A space opened up behind the ring where Sonny sat against the ropes as Byron pointed the gun at his head. 'I'm the king of the coal from now on.' He pulled the trigger.

The unmistakable sound of a pistol going off resonated in the air. But the blinding flash from the pistol as it backfired and blew up in Byron's hand shook and shocked everybody. The gun somersaulted out of his grip, breaking his forefinger and thumb He dropped on his knees to the canvas floor of the ring. Disorientated by the flash that had temporarily blinded him.

Sonny realised that he had stopped breathing for a few seconds and began sucking in a huge lungful of air. He desperately looked around for any of Byron's crew who would inevitably rush to his aid any second now.

Someone was rushing forward with a blade in his hand. It was Arthur, everyone had been searched as they entered the gym area to witness the spectacle, but they had missed the tiny razor-sharp penknife on his car keys that he normally used to cut the binding on the newspapers. He thrust his hands out of the ring and Arthur cut through the cable tie.

Sonny leapt up and got across the ring in a flash and smashed a right hand into the side of Byron's head. He was still on his knees, desperately trying to clear his eyes, holding his broken digits.

Byron had snorted up very nearly a quarter of an ounce mix of speed and cocaine that morning, and, as far as he was concerned, felt invincible. He sprung back to his feet in an instant and bull charged the younger man. Seeing what was coming, Sonny sidestepped and delivered another devastating hook to the other side of Byron's head. The second blow made him roar in rage at the audacity of the assault.

The six men who were with Byron including Marcus Evans, Sean Ramsey and Dave Wood, were given the look from certain powerful people in the crowd not to intervene.

Sonny set on Byron with frightening ferocity and a blinding rage. Reminding him with every blow of the names of the people that were being avenged. For nearly thirty minutes he battered the man around the eventually blood-soaked ring. Sometimes even hanging him up by his arms on the ropes, so he could pummel his head and body some more.

When Sonny finally stopped, all his energy was totally spent; his knuckles were bruised and bleeding and he stood in the middle of the ring at the extinguished body of Byron Lewis; the inevitable brain haemorrhage from the non-stop beating killing the drug fuelled maniac.

Sonny looked around the crowd. None of them looked shocked at what they had just seen. In fact, they looked with pride at the man who had got one over the devil. Peace was about to descend again around Mynydd Du. There was a Wilton back at the helm.

Arthur climbed into the ring and kneeled down at the bloody mess that was once Byron Lewis. He checked for a pulse and finding nothing gave a nod to four serious looking men in the crowd. They jumped in the ring and unfolded a large tarpaulin, originally meant to be Sonny's last shroud. They had taken it from Marcus Evans, who along with Sean Ramsey and Dave Wood had slipped away when they could see the castle was falling. Byron Lewis' body was soon wrapped up in the tarpaulin and dragged out of the ring.

Arthur put his coat around Sonny's shoulders and guided him to the ropes, where some other hands helped him out of the ring and onto solid ground. He made his way to the old log and sat down, looking at the ground, contemplating how close he had come to death. Arthur sat himself down next to him.

'It's over, Son, it's over, it's done.'

Sonny nodded in agreement, but he still stared at the floor. An old man came through the crowd, carrying a black briefcase.

He spoke very softly, 'Mr Wilton. My name is Alistair Buick from Buick and Mooney Solicitors and Accountants.'

Arthur raised a hand to the old gentleman, 'Not now please, my friend.'

'No, of course. I just wanted to announce my presence. I am officially retired but I have been taking care of the accounts and legal matters for Alf Wilton for over thirty years and continued to do so after my retirement. I shall be staying at this hotel and look forward to addressing the younger Mr Wilton on his very healthy financial position, when he is ready.' He handed a slip of paper to Arthur then turned and left, with two very large men providing his security.

The corpse of Byron Lewis was driven to Abbots Foundry that same evening and dropped into the huge melt furnace with ten tons of scrap iron. At around 1450 degrees. When all the iron has melted and, is ready for pouring, The dross is scraped from the top of the furnace and dumped to landfill, with all the other rubbish.

CHAPTER THIRTY-ONE
New Beginning

Sonny spent the next few weeks at the Hughes' house, in Rhian's bedroom. She remained downstairs in the front room, until her leg and arm were out of plaster. Apart from damage to his hands, a fantastic black eye and some bruised ribs, Sonny looked remarkably fit and healthy. With Arthur's support and Mrs Hughes' cooking and care, he finally began to relax his mind. Sleep became a little easier.

On the Thursday after the fight, Sonny took a walk up to the gym. The ring had gone. The canvas had been burned and the ring dismantled and returned to the boxing club. The whole area had been swept clean. There was no trace of what had happened two days before.

The next morning an appointment was made for 10.00am with Mr Buick in a small conference room at *The Valley Hotel* in town. Arthur accompanied Sonny as he trusted him implicitly to act as an advisor and confidante. His grandfather had written instructions on what was to happen to his wealth and businesses in a sealed journal, with the macabre title of Death or Disappearance. It was entrusted into the care of Alistair Buick. In it were the instructions for all scenarios. His death or disappearance, his and Beth's, and how he wanted his wealth donated if all three of them were to disappear or die.

'After some legal arguments I also managed to acquire all the paperwork that your grandmother was carrying the day she died,' Mr Buick said, addressing Sonny with genuine sympathy and respect. With a few signatures and sworn affidavits you will become the sole beneficiary of the estate of Alf Wilton. The monetary inheritance is as of today in excess of four million pounds.' Sonny nearly fell off the chair, and Arthur had a coughing fit and had to calm himself down.

'Your grandfather was an astute business man and first-class decision maker, Mr Wilton. There are still eight legitimate businesses varying from car repairs and sales, two public houses, a night club owned outright and another with shared ownership, and the provision of security to the social, hospitality and recreational industry that are still operating successfully today, with an annual profit of two million pounds after all deductions are taken out.' The old man leaned onto the office desk. 'There is also his vast property portfolio, excluding the villa and vineyard in Italy, equating to around three million if all properties were sold today.' He smiled at Sonny. 'Like I said, it's all yours after a few signatures and sworn affidavits. Unless you do actually know where Alf Wilton is, and that he is alive and well.' The last part of the sentence was spoken solemnly.

Sonny's' head dropped to the floor and he shook his head. What good would it do to bring it all out now? His grandfather was dead and buried under hundreds of tons of concrete. For his murder, their kind of justice had been done.

'You will, of course, have to find another loyal and trusted accountant and solicitor as I do actually intend to retire after this business is done. I shall call it my crowning glory and ride off into the sunset. After you have paid my huge fee, of course.' He laughed and stood up, offering his hand to both Sonny and Arthur. The meeting was over.

Outside, Arthur put an arm round the young man. 'Don't worry, we'll build you a team. Trusted and loyal. Old guard and new.'

Sonny smiled at his trusted advisor. 'Imagine, your daughter married to a millionaire businessman.' And walked away from Arthur.

Quickly chasing after him, Arthur joked. 'You haven't asked for my permission yet you cheeky bugger.'

DC Sharpe stood in front of Sonny, looking as if he hadn't slept well for a while. Scruffy and unshaven.

The office had been completely gutted, cleaned out and painted white, the lighting vastly improved. A brand-new set of filing cabinets stood behind a solid wooden desk and chair. The chair that had been on the front of the desk had been removed for this meeting. DC Sharpe was going to stand for his briefing. Arthur sat at another desk nearby.

'I now know that you did a lot of covering up, misdirecting and misleading all the investigations into both my grandparent's deaths.' Sonny spoke directly to the detective, and gave off the vibe that he didn't want, expect or need the man to deny, admit, or excuse his actions.

'And there is not a shadow of doubt in my mind that you would have done the same if Byron Lewis had got the better of me.'

DC Sharpe thought it best to say nothing. This young

man was coming across as someone who wouldn't wouldn't suffer fools gladly. Or liars.

Sonny reached into a small table next to him and dropped a folder on the desk. 'In there are details of practically every payment ever made to you? From when you worked for my grandfather, right up to the last five grand that Lewis gave you just a couple of weeks ago. Surprisingly, even he kept a record of your dirty money.'

The detective started to sweat and shuffled uncomfortably, especially at the mention of Alf Wilton, who had paid him well for merely turning a blind eye most of the time. *Not like that crazy bastard Lewis*, he thought. He wanted to murder and maim, then expect him to make it all go away.

'So, to prevent me from making all that information available to your seniors before you take your retirement, this is what you are going to do. You are going to do the same for me that you did for Lewis. You will steer away from me, all attention and suspicion for the disappearance of Byron Lewis. If the truth be known, the authorities will be delighted that he's gone, but still.' Sonny then stood and faced DC Sharpe looking at him hard. This police officer had no loyalty and would switch allegiance at the drop of a hat he thought to himself.

'Then when I'm satisfied that there is absolutely no threat to my liberty, you will take your retirement early because of your failing health. You can fuck off to that apartment in Spain that you've been paying for with your poisoned money. I will not hear of your presence in this part of the world again. Is that clear?'

The detective suddenly looked as if the sun had just come out. 'Yes, it is, Mr Wilton, and don't worry, there won't be a single copper at your door asking questions.'

Sonny nodded, and the detective couldn't get out of the office quick enough.

Patch drove from the barn down to Mynydd Du after Sonny phoned him to tell that all was well – that justice had been done. He invited him to the *White Hart*, a pub that Sonny would own once the legal issues had been dealt with. Sonny was beginning to employ managers and overseers that had been recommended to him by Arthur, or other trusted people from Alf's old circle. When Patch and Sonny came face-to-face again, they hugged like reunited best friends.

He knew that Patch wouldn't want the job of managing the security side of the business, but Sonny asked him if he could occasionally send a couple of guys or girls up there for his special training methods, especially the body guarding. Patch was only too happy to oblige.

A local builder, decorator, gardener and cleaning company were taken on to blitz the Wilton house. It was ready for Sonny to move into within a week.

He proposed to Rhian three months later. It was their first night out after she was out of plaster. She accepted, of course, and moved into the Wilton house. They married a year later, and they had twin boys, Thomas and Jacob, a year after that.

So began the reign of the next King of the Coal.

About the Author

After the death of his mother, Chris Kinsey was in the care system from the age of six until sixteen. He had no choice but to grow up fast and tough, and met some truly fantastic, dangerous, sad, and exciting individuals. Plus one or two lifelong friends.

Chris left Wales a few weeks before his eighteenth birthday. He said, 'I could see the downward spiral I was on and needed to extract myself from it or plummet to the bottom.'

Chris discovered that he had a strong work ethic and leadership potential, after finding work in the foundry industry. He continued this position until 2007, where plant closure and redundancy forced him to leave. He passed his heavy goods vehicle test that year, and spent the next five years behind the wheels of various lorries on a number of journeys.

He missed the camaraderie of industry work, so he successfully applied to join Jaguar Landrover in 2012 and continues to work there to this day.

Speaking of *A Dish Best Served Cold* he said, 'It has been a labour of love for me for a long time. A lot of the stories and plots are true happenings from my past, or stories told to me through the memories of friends in various stages of alcohol influence. I have enhanced some of those stories for effect. Due to having both knees replaced (Oct '17, May '18). I had the time to finally get it finished.'

Chris has been married to Hilary for fifteen years. He lives in Birmingham, and hopes to eventually retire near the coast, any coast.

.